Messaouda

ABDELHAK SERHANE

*translated from the French
by Mark Thompson*

CARCANET

First published in Great Britain in 1986 by
Carcanet Press Limited
208-212 Corn Exchange Buildings,
Manchester M4 3BQ

Carcanet
108 East 31st Street
New York
New York 10016

The publisher acknowledges financial assistance
from the Arts Council of Great Britain

British Library Cataloguing in Publication Data

Serhane, Abdelhak
Messaouda.
I. Title
843 [F]   PQ3989.2.S4

ISBN 0-85635-550-X

Typesetting by Koinonia Limited, Manchester
Printed in England by SRP Ltd, Exeter

For my mother, and for Manal, Hind and Tarik

Et je te dirais. . .
je te dirais l'exil
des jours lointains.

Translator's note

I am grateful to Paul Bowles, for his generous help with the spelling and meaning of Arabic words; and to Mark Ellingham, Paul Girolami, Michael Schmidt, and above all to Susan Daly, for their help and suggestions. M.T.

In the beginning was darkness, and in the beginning my fingers sketched the shape of a fallen woman: Messaouda. Two parallel lines, badly drawn; a single fine line; and a bulging black circle roughly finished with a few blots.

Messaouda the woman. Messaouda the man. Messaouda the animal. She was all three in one, the solitary hermaphrodite with a bat-wing tattoo on her sex. Silence itself flowed between her legs, and dreams became real. My grandmother used to say she was time's wound, and a trough for the adults who like pushing their fingers into her and tickling her withered breasts. She was one of those dark creatures who lie down and accept their own destruction. She was a fevered dream, spied out in the chaos of our vision and seized from our swooning clutch, from our failing, fainting youth by corrupt adults. Their terrible, mad frenzy found expression in her – frenzy of men who could not contain their climactic ecstasy.

The rest of us slept in a dream of her shadow, witnesses to the grinding scenes from a life laid bare and slung up on the hands of a silent clock.

Sometimes she shouted and screamed but she always ended with laughter in her toothless mouth, pushing her arse at the crowd while some of the men groped under her rags. We fantasized and clutched our pricks, unable to resist.

Sometimes the men had a good time stripping her or pulling her pubic hair, just to set her off, and they could always make her scream. Then she ran away weeping, chased by our brutal black hands and the grown-ups' cheers and laughter. She didn't stop till seized by other hands and pierced by other fingers, rank secretions always trickling out between her legs, fingers always digging into the labyrinth of her body.

7

We children looked on, caressing ourselves and remembering some other face or cleft.

So we learned about all life's inseparable gaiety and violence, and we absorbed the worst of it so young that it stained our memories. All of us had known the same call and the same cry. Later those voices burst and scattered in and around us, clearing the way for new lies and contradictions.

Messaouda went into every house but none belonged to her. The women used to wait for her to come. As soon as she had put down the buckets she had filled at Titahcen, they asked to hear her tales of suffering. They clustered round:

'Tell us what they did to you today!'

Then she was lost in her own awkward speech. Her tongue strained for lost words, raging like a fireball in her mouth while her arms smote the air meaninglessly. The women laughed. The girls listened. Their fantasies seemed to merge with our own. The girls gathered round the spring when Messaouda had gone, secretly touching themselves under their *haïks*, looking at each others' breasts and stroking their clefts.

Along with all the others, my father liked pushing himself against that ancient picture Messaouda kept between her legs.

To us she was the transparent woman, the eternal virgin, the flesh both tumescent and plundered. She was the cloudy figure with legs arched, always open to hairy fingers and avid eyes.

Messaouda the offering. Our lust's wound. The heavenly manna gorged by our elders. The entertainment that exposed the grown-ups' delirium and fertilized our forbidden pleasures.

The sinking sun was poised on the peak of Akechmir and our eyes widened like bubbles at the approaching darkness and flesh. We languished as we waited for Messaouda, thrilled to think she was naked under her robe.

It was enough for us that she sat down and parted her legs a little; enough for us to penetrate her with our stares, spittle on our hands and members erect. Our hands moved faster in bitter rhythm. We were blind with lustreless delight, freed for a moment from our anguish. We inhaled the odour of our efforts deeply from our sticky fingers. Now our hands looked almost like grown-ups', moistened in the swamp of Messaouda; and we were proud.

'Blessings be to God who gives pain. . .'. Messaouda imposed her own image on our fantasies, and we could conjure it ourselves for our pleasure. We were risking madness, tuberculosis, and sprouting hairs on the palms of our hands: a great risk, but our satisfaction was not to be denied. Messaouda laughed, cried, opened, closed and transformed herself. . . How we admired this woman/man/animal, offering herself so simply!

Thinking of the shape.
Seeing the shape.
Admiring the shape.
Penetrating the shape.

Our dream swelled and hugely overshadowed our despair. A glance from her was enough to make us mad with delight.
'Zib. . . Do you want some zib, Messaouda?'
She never answered – just laughed her black laughter – and the most daring ones didn't think twice about opening their trousers and displaying their members. Then she cried out sharply in wonder or disgust and fled along the streets, chased by the yearning erections of those valiant few. The crowd exploded with laughter. We were beaten, and realized with horror how very small we were.

Back home I shut myself in the lavatory, pulled out my scraggy member and set about reviving it; I was in a hurry to become a man and anyway, we had been taught that a man is worth the weight of his testicles. As soon as I let go, it sank down, quivering. A mere rag. I was weighed down with all the misery in the world. I found my school ruler. No progress. It was no less than despair at being an incomplete man.

'God created us equal,' my father often declared. I knew that was a lie because not everyone had access to Messaouda, the usufruct of the very adults who wounded her over again with the morality they peddled.

Messaouda the black androgyne was social inequality's stifling conscience, and the hurt done to God's word and us, the irony of a joyless life legislated by fate.

If we dared go closer, we were quickly chased off with a barrage of insults:

'Fiends! May God destroy you and your race!'

'Bastards! Have you ever seen such arrogance!'

'What an age this is, *Salama*!'

'These demons never give you any peace, in the name of God the Clement, Lord of Mercy!'

'I've heard they come from underground, *Yalatif*!'

'Get lost, bastards!'

'You've been damned since Adam and Eve!'

'A bunch of perverts! May God tear you out by the roots!'

Night came with its silence, bringing our voluptuous exile.

Your hand's violence
shaped my silence
And God's word made
my strangled sleep.

We woke in the morning with our bodies smelling of that woman – bodies we dragged heavily through a waking dream until the liberating moon rose again. So the thin line rejoined the line of time and the circle closed again around our obsession.

Now Messaouda's body was put in a cell. She became mere filth for our thoughts and looks, a blot on our reinstated virtue. Black by day and white at night, she partnered the moon, as she sailed on her pilgrimage through the fog of our fake piety.

Ramadan: a month's fast every year. Except for our fantasies we became pure from head to toe. We had to endure the pain of hunger, thirst and denial in the freezing winter or the summer heat. We succeeded through dignity and meditation, watched very closely by our parents who littered our lives with prohibitions, and when we were still very young locked us in a vicious framework of traditions and religious morality:

Don't smoke
Don't eat or drink
Don't fornicate
Don't think
Don't fart
Don't. . .
        Amen!
And Messaouda?

11

Don't touch her
Don't bruise her
Don't expose yourself to her
Don't look at her
Don't speak to her
Don't. . .
          Shit!

She was left in peace, and for a month we were freed from the sight of her while we went to the mosque with the grown-ups. We shared their meals and their prayers. We became shadows of their shadows: their faithful, obedient dogs. For that long moment we forgot the street orgies, the darkness of Messaouda, and the rank fluid seeping between her splayed legs. From time to time we sought refuge and relief in the lavatories, making sure our elders did not know. They were always on the watch, hoping to blame us for their explosions of aggression which were made all the worse by the Ramadan atmosphere of forgiveness and repentance.

'Where's Hafid?'

We were three attentive shadows, sitting cross-legged, forced to listen to our father spouting wisdom.

Mi was in the kitchen, heating and reheating the pan of lentils. It was the same every night, and Mi wept silently into her cooling lentils.

'God the Almighty said. . .'

But Hafid was on tenter-hooks: I knew Abdou was coming at ten o'clock, and Father was hardly likely to let him go.

'God said. . .'

A whistle echoed in the night: the agreed signal. Hafid had to go at any cost. I watched him carefully, knowing he was up to any trick that would let him recover his body's rhythm in friction or a clutching embrace.

In her dark kitchen Mi had had to reheat the lentils at least four or five times. The meal had to be ready whenever Father decided to eat, and neither too hot nor too cold.

'God said in his sacred book. . .'

Hafid used a moment's distraction on Father's part to put one of his tricks into operation. He stuck his finger down his throat and began vomiting on to the sheepskin.

'God said – shit! You're throwing up again, you pig! Get out, son of a bitch, get out! You always stuff yourself, so this is bound to happen. Get out of my sight, *qaouad*! Damn the mother who bore you!'

Hafid leaped up, hands clamped to his mouth. Father hurled a shoe at his back. Hafid was let off hearing the rest of the holy speech.

'Abdelhak, are you listening?'

Father's voice struck like a thunderbolt and smashed the silence that had briefly settled on the room. My father relished our exhaustion, our distress, our silent tears. In whose name was he tyrannising us?

In time Mi had grown used to her little life. It stretched behind her like old newspaper from the kitchen to the bedroom, a life full of trivia, and grounded in tears and pain. I even came to envy her patience and resignation, for Mi was a woman both patient and resigned.

'God said. . .'

Secretly and in silence, Hafid was shuddering behind Abdou's frail body. Then he'd come and curl up on Mi's lap. She would stroke his hair and tell him again the story of Mamma Ghoula or cunning H'didane. He would fall asleep dreaming of the full moon. O guilty innocence!

'God said. . .'

He hadn't said anything. Nor had Hafid said anything. He had got to his feet, wiped his face, jumped down the three steps, found a dark corner with Abdou, and reopened his body's wound.

'God said. . .'

The great silent clock struck midnight. My feet were hurting and my bottom ached.

Only four more days and Messaouda would be back again in all the desolation of her spurned flesh. A total of thirty days. Seven hundred and twenty hours. Then she'd be back, resurrected. . .

'God said. . .'

She would lift her rags, show her nakedness, open herself to fingers, metamorphose herself.

'God said. . .'

The grown-ups would overflow Messaouda. They would unleash their pricks. Their old hardened habits would return and we would look on as usual, powerless and silent.

On the night of *Qadr* we went with the adults to the mosque after supper. We stayed till dawn, waiting for the parting of the skies and the appearance of *Sidi Qadr*. Mouths prayed:

'*Sidi Qadr*, make me rich and healthy!'

'*Sidi Qadr*, I want my hair to be long and sleek like silk.'

'*Sidi Qadr*, send me to Mecca!'

'*Sidi Qadr*, restore my sight and the use of my legs!'

'*Sidi Qadr*, keep me to a ripe old age!'

Prayer begat prayer, breeding in pain and meditation.

'*Sidi Qadr*. . .'

The heavens remained indifferent to these deafening cries and piercing prayers.

All the *tolba*, all the *chorfa*, all the *fqihs*, all the good Muslims (and even the bad ones) had arranged to meet at the mosque on this night of absolution. What are a thousand months beside this night?

The Night of *Qadr*.

I was exhausted and finally dozed off on the damp matting. Next to me, Father was praying on the *kaaba*, designed in trompe-l'oeil on the red carpet that a relative had brought back from Mecca.

A man, in his prime and all in white, was descending from heaven. He rode a white mare. He held a shaft of light in his left hand and in his right, a ball of wool. He gathered the children to him, kissed each on the forehead, laid a little tuft of wool between their eyes and lifted them on to his mare. He met old men along the way and struck them with his ray of light, turning them into animals. In the mosque there were dogs, asses, rats, snakes, cats, pigs. . . My father had been turned into a monkey.

'Wake up and say your prayers, runt!'

There was a sudden stab of pain in my back. My venerable father had just roused me with a hard kick in the kidneys. I looked for my slippers but could not find them anywhere; they had disappeared.

'By the holy Moulay Driss and the holy Moulay Brahim, I ask *Sidi Qadr* to bless me with a prick like a bull and big balls, amen!'

The women were waiting and watching on the terraces outside. Mi waited, bare-headed: a living symbol. She repeated her supplication before going down to make the pancakes for the *s'hor*.

'*Sidi Qadr*, forgive my sins old and new, and deliver me from the hell you've thrown me into!'

Back home, my father said his last prayers, hurriedly told his prayer-beads, undressed, put out the light, and penetrated Mi in the dismal silence. It was Mi's duty to keep quiet and accept the penetration. She was a woman and had no right to sexual pleasure. Mi was a chaste and virtuous wife, not a whore. She was the vessel in which father relieved himself when he could not fulfill his fantasies in the brothels.

Then, a lull.

The great clock hands followed time's monotonous course. When Messaouda returned, the grown-ups were less concerned about us and more with their genitals. God stopped speaking altogether. He grew deaf and dumb, and his sacred word was put on the shelf beside the prayer-beads and the prayer-mat. God no longer said anything at all. And Messaouda returned with the returning darkness.

During the holiday, the fine line was drawn before our eyes. We were clothed, given pocket money or a piece of cake, and sent into the street to scoop up ecstasy in our cupped hands.

'O God, save us from shipwreck!'

15

After the month of Ramadan, piety took its leave and tongues grew venomous again. What could people do in a small town where the walls were stained with grief and rouged over with lies and crime? – They could talk. And harsh words spared no one. The men sat slandering in the shop-fronts all day.

'Here comes H'lima the water-carrier. She has the evil eye – God protect us!'

'She's a bastard, what do you expect?'

'Did you know she was married once?'

'Yes, her husband was a true gentleman. She killed him inch by inch because she wanted his house.'

'Yes, but it wasn't his house. It belonged to his sister in Beni Oulid.'

'I don't like to criticize but she only got what she deserves.'

'Haddou the tanner is back from Tangier.'

'That old drunk – we'd only just got rid of him.'

'And he said he'd found work.'

'He's a liar! Who knows if he ever *went* to Tangier?'

'Don't worry, he'll certainly show us all his train ticket.'

'That's no proof.'

'I don't like talking about things that are none of my business but believe me, he doesn't deserve any better. . .'

All day long this sneering gossip thrived among us and we on it. Neither my father nor I were let off; people started their slanging as soon as we appeared in the street.

'Si Driss, your pet monkey's a honey-lover!'

'And it eats shit out of your mother's cunt, you whore's son, you son of a bitch, you son. . .'

My father – so big, so strong, so domineering – had a phobia about honey. Admittedly it was only a game, like Messaouda:

16

a permanent game. Game-playing was obligatory because hypocrisy was everywhere, and my father played well. With his acting-up about honey he had wrapped himself in a cloak of good-will. He was nicknamed 'Honey' and I, by logical deduction, was called 'Son of Honey'. It was only a game to him, but my dignity suffered and I was so disgusted with everything that I wanted to die.

'Well, good day to you, Honey boy.'

'Where's Honey, your father?'

'Aren't you going to give us some honey like the bees?'

All the sniping made my head spin. Their sarcasm spoiled my solitude and spurred my hatred. This new humiliation was refined with each passing day, and it disgusted me to have to put up with it. How hard to be a child in an adults' world! Pride would not let me degrade myself to the level of this crew, and I managed to keep my balance in the midst of their malice. I fought back with my indifference.

When my father spoke, I climbed back into my own remotest past to try and identify him – to discover where I first met him. He was lost in my oldest childhood memories. My father, the stranger! Then I tried to draw him towards my sympathy, to locate him among the happiest things of my life, but he escaped and slipped away, planting himself in the darkness of my indifference.

In the mysterious night-time streets, Messaouda wandered through my restless dreams. I lusted for her with each throb of memory, and raped her in the streets in full view of the others, who were helpless; while my father slept, lapped in his sloth and my hatred.

Messaouda the insult had returned. Her hole, our redeemer, lurched about in the labyrinth of our lives. It was dark and a bit damp, and it was hurt trying to resist the stubborn fingers and erect members, already drunk on the smell of her secretions. It was always sleeping around, always open and ready for the grown-ups.

17

I awoke in the morning, bitterness between my legs. Father swaggered, bawled, spat, swore, lashed out – and we submitted. The monkey encouraged Father's spewing flow. It was particularly shameless and seemed to approve whatever its master and protector did. Only Messaouda persevered in her orbit of erotic hunger. At night the town shut its doors again. The men tied up their trousers and Messaouda shut up her sex. Only the monkey was left. It had to be killed as soon as possible.

I wondered: 'Do all children feel the same pain as me? Are my problems like theirs? Are my deprivations the same?'

Father no longer loved Mi. Had he ever loved her, though? To him, love was a weakness. So he did not love his children, or anybody else, or anything that was worth loving. He never loved what should or could be loved: so he loved his monkey: a grotesque injustice but a cunning one, meant to grind us down still further. The chamberpot under Father's bed was always full and had to be emptied every morning. That was one way of humiliating us – making us carry his urine and inhale the sickening smell of that visceral hatred. Ours was a cruel fate. Father himself was frightened of the cold air and never left his room at night.

The walls closed around Mi the day Father ordered her out of his bed and into our room. She was his trough and second chamberpot.

'The children are growing up fast,' he announced one day. 'From the point of view of their education it's bad that you still sleep in the same bed as me. Go to them, wife! You should be looking after them. I'll let you know when I need you.' Then we were isolated with Mi: she in her solitude and we in our uselessness.

Mi accepted the new affront without flinching. She was submissive and resigned; a submissive, resigned cow. Mi was a factory for making children, a machine to keep house, and an instrument for relieving Father's swollen member. And he made demands on her generosity nearly every night. She won back her place as soon as the signal came, and then returned to loneliness and exile with us. Our walls coffined her. The cards were on the table.

But there was still the monkey.

I wanted to strangle it, disembowel it, string it up. . . but why did it always make me think of Father? I could not see it without its turning into a monkey with a man's head – my father's. Father as a monkey with a man's head, or a man with a monkey's head.

When the right moment came to finish it off, I girded myself and stole a brand new razor-blade from Father's drawer (kill it with his own blade!). I could count on Hafid's silent support. Entranced, I went to it: there was nothing to fear, nothing to lose anymore. I knew I would kill it and braced myself by repeating over and over, 'It must die!' It only needed one cutting stroke: such a simple action. Its blood would spring out and certainly splash the walls. The living insult would be gone. Its blood would congeal and its remains fall away into silence and oblivion. All of us, Mi, Hafid and I would be released.

I was near the end of my pilgrimage. My stomach was already convulsed with anguish. Suddenly I hesitated: I'd lost the strength to act out my desires alone. Was it cowardice? The act itself and my deliverance were at my fingertips. All it needed was an arm raised and then lowered. But there was too much night around me, and too much loneliness. It wasn't a question of making plans: if we were to get rid of the animal, I had to be hard, had to know how to find my way through black madness. I was frightened of getting its blood on my hands, and not at all keen on having dirty hands at my age. But I had not given up – I couldn't: I was the others' hope. My arm dropped to my side. For the moment my courage had failed hopelessly, collapsed in mid-flight. I would have to start again. Now I was worn out.

And the monkey was still there.

It survived all my efforts, like sin itself. It was an insult and a challenge that poisoned my heart. Was I incapable of settling the miserable thing's fate? I was certain I could do it eventually:

19

I would prevail! It would die before my very eyes and I'd rejoice. Its death alone could free me.

And the monkey was still alive.

And my hatred and pain, more precious than blood, were still alive too. There was enough hate in me to annihilate the whole world; injustice had been the air I breathed and I learned to be unjust in my turn. Father had taught me to despise women when he carried me about as a kid on his back, and Mother had never concealed her contempt for men. I was torn between those incompatible passions and became a misanthrope in spite of myself.

Father continued to swagger, belch and roar, relishing his brutality, spitting, swearing, hitting out. . . And we submitted.

The wind had dropped, no longer keeping us company with its murmur. We lived in suspense, hanging from the great clock hands. Even time had stopped passing; it was put aside. It hung on Father's erratic moods, clung to him like a snarling dog. Our life stank of monkey, putrid water, incessant fighting, crabbed desire, shame and humiliation.

I hated the chamberpot, and my plans were hopelessly becalmed. I would have to empty it every morning for ever, and every morning I longed to make him drink the lot, or at least empty it over his head. That would have been some consolation; my monkey-headed father would have become my piss-headed father.

But night extinguished all hope of revenge. I was paralysed by fear of my father – fear of his fury – and would have to be very careful.

Mi usually relieved herself in a large chamberpot: she was terrified of the dark pit. I could taste salt in my mouth when I heard Mi urinating. She pissed like a cow. I imagined her doing it when I was alone. Was she like Messaouda? Did she exude the same odour? Was there dried sperm on her buttocks too? And what about her hole? I tried to picture it. I gave it every shape I knew: a split black olive, a crooked knee, a delicate pear, the curving juncture of lips, a shapeless stew, a juice-gorged raspberry, a cracked wall, and – why not? – a roaring mastiff's head. I tried them all but wanted to imagine it as it really was: a mess, just like Messaouda's. I had trouble giving it exactly the shape it deserved. I could scarcely picture Mi's sex at all and could not find a truthful image. Mi's sex was definitely not like any other. It was unique: and it was through it that I had fallen on my hard times.

The monkey was still there.

And there was still pepper, too. Mi always said that indifference was the best way to kill someone. But as the monkey was not 'someone' it would have to die some other way. It was embarrassed by our indifference but not at all disturbed; it was used to our silence. So it must be forced out of its intolerable serenity. What could I do to provoke it?

Hafid was sitting in a corner, fondling himself under his *djellaba*. He thought no one could see. Mi was praying on the sheepskin rug which had received me at my birth. Messaouda was probably asleep under a parched tree, legs spread wide, her hole gaping. I pictured all the beasts of the earth penetrating her as they would a jungle: a monkey, a squirrel, a rat, an elephant, a hedgehog. . .

Messaouda was asleep and felt nothing. Her sex-cavern was no longer hanging out of her. A lizard, if it was too long, could have left its tail dangling out. Messaouda awoke with a jump, came down into the town and knocked on every door, asking each man if he had left his prick in her. The men answered with a smile and felt their groins, made sure everything was present and correct, shut their doors, did up their trousers and went back to sleep. There the dream stopped. Anyway it was cold, and I couldn't dream any more.

Beware the cold night air!

Father was sneezing, and the monkey too. He must have caught a cold or inhaled some pepper. How funny a monkey is when it sneezes! All its wretched animal stupidity was in its sneezing. I had him this time. I knew what I must do. My hatred was big enough to destroy a whole planet. The animal was defenceless before my anger; courage had nothing to do

21

with forgiveness any longer, and I grasped every chance to persecute the vile creature. Pepper only made it sneeze: I had to find something else, something worse, something atrocious. So I made it drink the dregs of red wine from the bottles strewn under Father's bed. It got drunk, make ridiculous noises, capered about grotesquely, somersaulted, scratched its arse, threw up and rolled on the floor. I discovered a new sort of disgust: revulsion for beings infinitely oppressed, alone and small.

Mi pissed her bitterness into her chamberpot. The pungent liquid splashed on the cracked sides with a strange sound, like water at the bottom of a well.

All my thoughts were concentrated on the monkey. What if I cut off its sex? Why not burn it alive in the fire? There was no hurry; all of time stretched before me. To bring this off I'd have to organize myself properly – choose the right time. For the time being it was more important to make it suffer slowly, calmly, scrupulously. I had undertaken to make it suffer and was succeeding very well. After the pepper and alcohol, I made it eat laxatives all day long. He would never take it to the vet – gossip had to be avoided. Diarrhoea all day long, stinking so badly in Father's bedroom that he was forced to put the unworthy animal out on the terrace. Then it was alone with my hatred. There was no escape from my ferocity, day or night. Its diarrhoea flowed like a stream; it could not avoid the terrible fate I had reserved for it. Its end was at hand.

Morale at home was higher than before, and Mi found her smile again. 'God is great,' she would say, 'God is merciful.' She ignored or pretended to ignore the fact that I was responsible for the good deed. She gave me twenty centimes the day the monkey departed the bedroom for the terrace. She began to trust me again and gave me her blessing several times a day. Her encouragement sharpened my hatred and fuelled my violence. The ominous beast was going to succumb at last, and in the darkest circumstances. Its carcass would tumble into silent oblivion and we would be free.

Only Father would weep. He wept for everything that was

not worth his tears. He went straight to the terrace when he was home from work, to check the health of his 'other half' before presenting his heavy hand for us to kiss. His smell mixed with the monkey's stink and made me feel sick. Father would weep for sure! And seeing Father's weakness would make every trouble and sacrifice worth while. This desire grew stronger and stronger. I was tormented by a sort of pride: nothing could withstand God's will – or mine.

Its imminent downfall cheered me up. It become more and more repellent, more and more beastly, more and more abject; which was just what I wanted. And each day the image of my father superimposed itself on the animal's features. Sometimes the two got confused, and then I was sorry for the monkey.

This little merry-go-round could have lasted even longer, but I had had enough. The game had stopped being funny. But then, if I brought it off, I would have nothing more to do. That would have been the end of it.

Strangely, the image of Messaouda had come to occupy a position between the other two. It was no joke; I no longer knew which image to smash: Messaouda, the monkey and my father filed together through my memory and I couldn't separate one from another. Messaouda was indispensable to my fantasies and I still clung to her: it was not a good moment to banish her from my life. Luckily a Frenchman appeared in time to put a stop to this; he offered Father money for the animal, and from that point the three images separated in my mind.

I always dreaded that feeling of emptiness, of not having any supreme reason for existing. Now I was face to face with the fact of my own nullity. I felt I had reached the end of my own sad journey through savagery, and was swallowed up in a sort of disgust. It was not pleasant!

O remorse! I longed to wail at the vulgarity of my defeat and my untimely pride.

I welcomed the night in my anguished bed, and with it the complicity of silence, humiliation and impotence.

And within me the bee lived on.

Read, in the name of the Lord
Who made man from the void!
Read!. . .
For your Lord the Most Generous
taught man all manner of calamity
taught him all that he ignored

How can I explain what was happening to me? Messaouda vanished among my memories, and her sex slipped from my memory. There was no room for her or it in my new life. It was a new adventure, paved with lies: my body and my memory were being taken over by words, Body and memory were two negations suspended from the harshness and monolithic truth of sixty *hizb* – the hundred and forty *surat* which I had to be able to recite faultlessly.

His black eyes caught me one morning, on the terrace. I knew the punishment would be formidable: a well-aimed *falaqa* and house arrest for a few days, solitary confinement for several weeks, a hundred lashes on my back, pecks of burning pimento or black pepper on my lips. . . To my amazement, there was nothing of the sort. But at dawn the next day, Father hauled me like a sack of potatoes to the feet of a withered, taciturn old man. I didn't dare look up. The *fqih* hit me over the head with the knob of his stick, which was an olive branch. Father gave him a detailed account of my behaviour, sparing none of his deep disappointment and advising him to deal severely with me. The *fqih* called for the two biggest and strongest of his pupils. They lifted me bodily from the ground, wedged my feet between the rope and the plank, and the honourable master administered the obligatory *falaqa* under my

24

father's satisfied gaze. Before leaving me to my fate he roared from the doorway of the gloomy building:

'This cur is no longer my son. Now he's yours. You'll get some money every Thursday and I won't forget holidays. I'm relying on you to educate him. If you can't shake him out of his idleness and insolence, kill him, and I'll come and bury him.'

So I entered the Koranic school, and time soon revealed the meaning of his words. I was buried alive.

It was hard for Mi to accept the new arrangement. It was another check on her, another demonstration of her insigificance. What could she do? Neither talismans nor charms nor magic words could get me out of this pass. There was no way I could escape Father's will; nor did I have any doubt I would soon be dead, or any difficulty in weeping in self-pity. No more carefree playing: no more childhood!

I was the earth's accursed, the vicious character who had to be kept far away, bridled and out of sight at any price. And I was the weakest.

I spent all God's days sitting cross-legged on a damp, foul-smelling mat, flanked by other children from the quarter, chanting, beating the polished wooden board with my fists, silently weeping, saying the same words over and over, mechanically, hundreds of times, being martyred. So, I repeated over and over, interminably, silently, the pedantic early-morning lessons dictated by the honourable *fqih* of the *m'sid*. In the evening I rattled them off to him, hung my board back on its nail, said the last prayer, kissed his hand and went home, deafened by the holy words still buzzing in my head, drained by the effort I had to make every day. I fell asleep as soon as I got home.

My father was pacing in the dense night, the monkey on his right shoulder. His footsteps stupefied me, deafened me. I shadowed him like a dog. From time to time he looked round to make sure I was suffering. The monkey pulled faces at me.

After centuries of walking, Father stopped, took a length of wet rope out of his pocket and tied my hands together. The monkey hopped on to my back. Father pulled me over the wet sand by the rope binding my fists. I wept and suffered, Father tugged, I wet myself, Father pulled, I vomited, Father pulled, I choked, Father pulled. . .

Second scene: Father on his feet with the monkey back on his shoulder. A withered tree in the middle of a huge, barren landscape. A rope with a slip-knot.

The monkey jumped down and scampered up the tree. Father took off his white *djellaba* and laid it on a rock. He said a prayer where he stood, went over to the tree and threw one end of the rope up to the monkey, which tied it to a branch. I just watched. Eventually he seized me and looped and fastened the rope around my neck. Before I knew what was happening I was swinging between heaven and earth, howling, weeping, screaming, thrashing about, threatening, swearing, begging. When I had no strength left, I calmed down. A man in white emerged from the darkness, came straight for me and tore off my trousers. He brandished a long rusty carving knife, and cut off my sex with one slash. Blood spurted. The man tossed the bit of flesh to the monkey. Blood was running freely. The animal gobbled it up. The blood ran. I wept. My blood gushed. Father offered up a second prayer. The blood was surging. Father cut me down. My blood was still streaming. Father panicked and fled from my blood, which rose higher and higher. . . Father was running, the blood was rising. Too late. He didn't even have time to shout. He was already drowned in my blood.

Unbearable grief hunched, balled, in my stomach. I knew that was what my father had always wanted. I sobbed helplessly, my tears rolling on like a river and disappearing into the red waves of my night. The monkey dived into the tepid blood, surfaced behind Father and brought him back to shore like a stranded boat. His body was already limp as a rag.

A cold hand was pressing on my sweating forehead. I opened my eyes: it was Mi. She had woken me up – it was

26

time to go to the *m'sid*. I was exhausted, and reached down to my groin. My penis was hot to the touch: it was there, definitely there and alive. I stroked it under the blanket, teased it, grasped it tightly in my hand: and if Mi hadn't been there, I'd certainly have hugged and roused it to ejaculation to prove its sound working order. It was so tense and nervous that my stomach hurt. I was almost proud of it.

I was circumcised soon afterwards, and that threw more light on my nightmare. Father chose Tatour the barber to drive me across the swamps of childhood blood. His scissors glinted: my head swam.

Our neighbour Lalla Kenza was sterile. Mi gave her my newly-cut prepuce to eat. A year later she had her first baby.

Circumcision deprived me of all the privileges of childhood. Till now I had always gone to the Turkish baths with Mi. Unlike the other children my age, I was happy there: bathing days were holidays to me.

'Watch me and learn how to wash yourself properly, runt!'

Crouching in front of me, Ba Driss was washing. I imitated him. His thick penis hung down to the ground. The sight of it made me giddy. I reached down to my own and couldn't find it at all: it had shrivelled up in shame before its senior. Si Driss was obviously proud of his. For a moment I saw imaginary shapes in the shadows, vague forms in motion, graceful and erotic. Suddenly the image of Mi arrived, dispatched the rest, and took sole charge of my imagination. I felt my scarred bit of flesh suddenly swell between my legs, and went into the lavatory to catch the hot neuroses of my incestuous childhood in my hand.

The fact that I would not be going back to the women's *hammam* hurt me. I was a man now, and the women were modest enough to tell tales to the *tayaba*, the huge supervisor at the baths. We were getting ready to leave one day when she called Mi and told her in a nasty voice that I couldn't come to the women's baths any more.

27

'The next time,' she added, 'we'll get hold of your lord and master, and the women will be very happy to wash his balls for him.'

This cut was meant for me. I realized the women who used to lust after me had seen that my penis was heavier and my looks less appealing than before. Circumcised, I was no longer a child to them: I had to abandon my childhood precisely when, for the sake of my sexual development, I most needed its mysteries. At that time my whole life revolved around a single image – that of Mi. The unwanted one was ejected, banished from the world of the Arabian Nights, and plunged without warning in a world where all caressing and gentleness were forbidden. Because of my wound I must now find my way again, from one day to the next, in an extremely arduous, essentially masculine world. I was a man amongst men! This banishment signalled the beginning of my wanderings: dream gave way to reality, high spirits to hostility, childhood to – a blank. I had to change my ways completely – had to get used to new genitals in new surroundings and learn to bear myself like a man in my new, forced exile.

The new atmosphere was crushing me, and I fought with all I had not to sink into madness. Everything at the men's baths pushed me towards homosexuality. I was always afraid to be there by myself; naked men were always prowling, waiting for a new arrival so they could scar his body with their violent desire. They'd get him between their legs on the pretext of soaping his back and, before he knew what was happening, he was their lacerated victim.

As soon as Mi had undressed me, I hid in the warm, wet, thick steam. My eyes soon adjusted to the light and I glanced around, assessing the talent before setting off on my erotic quest through the groins which the women, as was their custom, were depilating or shaving: neat, clean cunts to stimulate male fantasies. Some of them had erotic tattoos.

Then my attention strayed from crotch to crotch, from breast to breast, and I grew excited, and ravished the sweet shadowy shapes with my gaze. My prick was inflamed by the pungent smell of women and strained between my legs, every movement shuddering through me to the tip of my body. The situation encouraged secret masturbation: quick, delicate hands went to and fro on the women's moist bodies, which were oiled and softened by steam, soap and *ghassoul*. My longing to penetrate every one of them made me increasingly sad, so I sent my prick off to seduce the dark soft figures. It went into one hole, came out, around another, teased a third, sucked on a breast, stroked another, came back to me, went off again to tickle some thigh or other. . . The women wriggled and laughed at it. Back in the fray, it penetrated another sweetheart, hurried back out, switched direction, climbed on to a truly magnificent thigh, sidled into a hairless hole and loitered there. I became impatient. My desire grew huge and long, and sprouted roots. I called it to heel. It came back out drunk with pleasure and vomited the rest of its fantasies on to the firm thigh. My hand collected the scourings of my delight.

A succulent hell! And the sounds? – I contained them all. I listened and spied on them the better to possess them: sound of water, sound of buttocks, sound of tongues, sound of genitals. . . And the smells? – Smell of henna, smell of sperm, smell of *ghassoul*, smell of virginity. . .

My anguish gradually burned itself out, and the sounds and smells in me were extinguished as I grew used to hard genitals. Thus I buried my childhood at the other end of the world, buried a truth which consisted essentially of breasts, genitals, buttocks, and a few dreams.

This was the troubled subsoil – my childhood – where I sowed my songs of blood and sperm.

Prayer, prayer – don't ask more of the slaves
than they can give.
As to your women, fear God – fear God

The words came to occupy part of my body. By force of repet-
ition they bred in my memory and made my head ache. I was
scarcely more than an infant, and there were beatings as well
as words. One day I decided to stop the massacre.

I had already been warned that 'The *fqih* is your father,
mother, teacher and protector from hell.' Our *fqih* was indeed
our father, mother and defender from hell; which was a lot.
During the day he taught us holy religion. In the evening he
sheltered us under his *djellaba*. He protected us from the disturbing silence, and was the first to cut the scar of despair in
our bodies. He took the youngest ones on his lap and filled
their frail bodies with his paroxysms. But he never gasped:
just closed his owl eyes as he shuddered on the brink of blasphemy.

One Thursday night, after the last prayer, I stayed behind
to sweep out the building and let old age penetrate my flesh.
I was alone with the *fqih*. I wasn't afraid of being betrayed by
some tactless friend, now, because I didn't confide in any one.
Two days before I had gathered some 'camel's cheek' by myself
– a hallucinogenic plant well known in Azrou by the name of
tabourzighte. Only the good seeds, black and dry. I put two
handfuls in the little teapot and let it boil. Meanwhile the old
man was praying. Before he could call me under his protection,
I drained the pot into a large glass which he drank off straightaway. He soon grew drowsy. I put him to bed and went
home. Towards midnight we were wakened by shouting. The

30

old man was outside, naked in the night, chattering and yelling, capering and leaping about like a plucked cockerel. His genitals jigged to and fro. People came to their windows, outraged by his enormous lies:

'. . . I'm a spider, a black spider in your children's bodies. I'm only a child myself, badly wrinkled by the sun – the lie goes in one ear and out the other – just laughter's left. . . I've got a pass to Paradise – yesterday I had a visit from Aïcha Qandischa – I think I was praying at the time – she took me by surprise. . . that fire in my throat, it's come a long way. . . call me H'matchas and Issaouas, I want to dance, want to go into a trance and smash your skulls with my axe. Are you laughing? I'm not J'ha and I'm not the bastard H'diddane – I tell you I'm the black spider with an ivory prick. . . come under my skin, find peace and repentance – welcome me and my solitude, you're my friends and brothers – come to me, my slaves, come around and yield to my words – they will be kind to you. Bring down your women so I can get a better look at them, those women with a thousand and one secrets, those paragons wearing the mark of my lie as a charm – I'm their miracle-worker, they always open themselves to my lies. . . I'm not raving, I'm not mad, not yet – truly I've just recovered – coming back from far away with my reason. . . my nights are calmer. . . here is the key – I'm resigning, getting out of the camel's camp to greet the dove again. . . that's only the start – tomorrow I'll be there when you rot, no question about it, and I'll put your scars into bottles or plastic bags – whichever you prefer. . . I bring you new differences in the wake of new violence – I come from far away to free you from the ants boring into your dreams. . . I come to ravage your fantasies and lock them in chaos with your own shit. . . I bring you the sun in one hand and words in another – I come to plant a plaster mask in your faceless earth and on your history so compromised by fate, and your stormy new fate – I bring you hope of a new immaculate sex to put under your pillow and bring riches, glory, love and madness. . .'

People closed their windows again. The words outside smelt

31

of sweat and blasphemy. Mi was listening behind the door. Father was saying his prayers and spitting into the neck of his *t'chamir*, a loose nightshirt that reached his knees.

When all the windows were shut the children crept out into the night and went to the old man. His words slid along the dark streets and rapped on half-asleep consciences. We were all there around him and listened very keenly.

'Everything's false, everything's a lie. I'm your father, my children, I'm the word that never fails. . . leave your slates and join me in peace – follow me for eternal truth. Take your pricks in hand and admire the magma of breasts probing the sky – I'm the freedom and truth that no one ever teaches you – I'm the clock of last judgement – I'll chime for them. . . terror and anguish. . . and I'll have you hidden away by the heavenly angels. Fear nothing, fear no one – my prayers are with you – come, my children, follow me – follow me!. . .'

We were leaving the town, the old man at our head, chattering and gesticulating. The children clapped their hands and chanted a children's rhyme over and again:

O *fqih* Bouzakri
The maddest aren't prisoners
The cleverest aren't heard
The baddest are gaolers
The richest aren't lenders
The middling aren't the last
The blessed are like Bouzakri

Though it was very late the children escorted their master and protector, who wandered, lost, into the shadows of the cemetery.

The *fqih*'s resignation was as sudden as unexpected, and I did not go back to the *m'sid*. Father had started to distrust holy writ and gave me into the care of the school mistress. It was another way of getting rid of me and punishing me. The school mistress never ate in class. I can't say anything much against her. The *fqih* went permanently mad because of a few cursed seeds. I think I overdid the dose a little.

The mistress was nice, and we gazed raptly at her large bosom. New words replaced the word of God, and slates made way for books. We were exempted from rejoining the dawn on the parallel line of time. And we were let off prayers and hand-kissing. We liked to hold Madmouzille's delicate fingers (she always wiped them straight afterwards with a moist handkerchief) in our grimy hands. How much richer our fantasies the day the wind blew up her checked skirt in the playground! After that there was no room in my head for anything except the shimmering image of her perfect white legs.

I was already on the dangerous brink of adolescence and sensed another personality taking shape within me, sensed an expert, invisible hand controlling and transforming my body. I was becoming someone else.

Messaouda could spread her legs and Mi could piss in the chamberpot: their movements and noises did not touch me now, for I was in search of a new sound and shape for my new wound. I found them in class, watching her every move, and lost in what I saw. I used to drop my pen when she came towards me, looking for a glimpse up and under.

Mi waited every day to take me on her lap and comfort me while she told the story of her life.

'I was young, very young when your father married me. . .'

When Mi started to resurrect her memories, I had to abandon my own daydreams and concentrate.

'I was only just fourteen. I'd just had my first periods. . .'

Pretending was out of the question: it was my duty to listen, interrupt, gasp with amazement, and sometimes swear. Somehow I had to live through her desperate past with her, minute by minute, and be her echo.

'I was beautiful and still a child. . .'

O God, spare me from sleep and exhaustion!

'Your monster of a father was ten years older than me. . .'

Each night, Hammada came along and settled himself beneath our window, saying meaningless things that would have made the dead blush, spitting on the ground, pissing in the middle of the street, swearing and cursing.

'I'd never met him before, never seen. . .'

Hammada must have been angry that night: he was shouting, 'God hasn't been respected. . . the helmets have fallen. . . *Zib* was there and saw it all – he wept over the spilt blood – my balls cleaned up the rest. . .'

Hammada was leaning against our wall as usual, speaking truths which fell on the ground and were crusted over by the street dust. Mi worked ceaselessly at her words to make them express her despair:

'On our wedding night, your ghoul of a father came into my bedroom, tore off my veil and trousers and. . .'

Hammada had stopped. He was probably looking for his *sebsi* at the bottom of his sack. After the *fqih*, his pipe was the only thing he really took seriously and had any respect for. Silence and tension. His voice rang out again.

'Hammada knows everything, Hammada says everything – everything that worries you. I'm mad, I'm free and I shit on you – you deserve no better, you dung-hill. You're not worth a fart to Hammada Bouizargane. . .'

Time had stopped in this corner of the world, underlining Hammada's naked words. Mi continued:

'He was so brutal that I panicked. They said he had killed one of his enemies. He threw himself on me like a starving animal. He grappled with me for hours. At dawn he still hadn't penetrated me: I was clenched tight. People outside were asking questions about my virginity and his virility. Then your father went out, ate a meal of honey and almonds, and came back with Lalla M'barka the corpse-washer. She smeared my sex with olive oil and spread my legs wide towards your father. I fainted just after that and your father was not there when I came to. The sheet and my bloodstained trousers were hanging from a nail above my head. That night I lost whatever value I'd had. . .'

A grin spread across Mi's lips. I writhed with grief. She still had the strength to smile. I looked down at my feet: they were

frozen and dirty. Hammada's words unrolled across the night:
'This is Hammada speaking, Hammada your Lord and Conscience. . . blood has flowed, the sheep has bleated and blood,
I tell you blood has flowed, red blood, human blood. The
wounded bird still flies its distant flight, far from the world
of shame and corruption. The helmets are abandoned in the
market-place, the end is at hand. . . Laugh, good people, since
you laugh easily – laugh! laugh! Who lives will weep. I was at
the waterfront for the first time and I've seen what I've seen
– I've seen hatred and misery – seen the shabby dream of a
people curled up in the scar of my memory – seen your history
smashed on the bleak stones. . . Laugh, good people, laugh!'
Damn! I was completely forgetting that Mi was going to
great lengths to convince me of the tragedy of her existence.
'I thought I had a man,' she was saying. 'A man to help me
bear my burdens, a man who would listen and share my
sorrows, a man worthy of what I'd tell him. . .'
'Don't stop, Mother, I'm listening!'
She turned her head and furtively wiped away a tear running
down her cheek. I was sorry for the trouble I had given her.
Hammada was a permanent feature of Azrou. His madness
was carved in time and space. He thought he was the king of
the forest. He loved the trees and birds and even claimed he
had inherited them from his grandfather: the forest was *his*
forest. Everyone in Azrou knew Hammada Bouizargane: the
only man who dared to denounce social injustice in public.
He was forgiven; he was mad.
'Keep silent, good people, and stay that way if you're scared
of talking. God will provide. Be what you are: cowards from
head to toe. . . but *I* refuse to be yours. . .'
He was right under our window. Mi stopped talking for a
moment. Hammada's voice filled my head till I thought it
would burst. I began to be afraid.
'Stay silent, good people! You are only good for that. What
goes up must come down, that's nature's law – the black
Demon of hate has climbed very high in the sky. Don't be like
him, good people – he will fall one day, and what a crash there

35

will be. . .'
He beat the ground with his stick to emphasize his points, took out his prick and pissed against our wall. Mi blushed. I lowered my eyes. Mi took up again, in the same desolate voice:
'The next morning my blood went round the town on a silver plate. I had just locked the belt of legitimacy round my life and saved family pride. Our honour was safe. . .'
People cutting wood in the forest were more frightened of Hammada than of the warden. Had he not murdered Si Hida with an axe, over a stick of green wood? The authorities blamed the murder on his madness and Hammada was very soon back among his trees and birds. Apparently there was an arrangement between the law and the forestry officials.
'Teach your children, good people, and unmuzzle your women. Remember, you good people, remember, you sons of the top men, that if I'm illiterate it is because I wasn't allowed an education – my name is Hammada *Ben* Moh and not Hammada *Ou* Moh. Remember good people, every road leads to Azrou, but to the French, I was just on the fringe of the Berber lands. Be quiet and keep quiet. . .'
Hammada had sat down. I guessed where he was by the racket he made, beating the ground with his staff. Mi listened, secretly looking at me; then she lowered her voice and eyes, and continued:
'Brutal. Yes, your father was a brutal man, a monster. I used to go out once a month to the *hammam* and once a year to worship at the tomb of Sidi Ben H'midane. Wherever I went, his sister came too: I wasn't allowed out anywhere alone. . .'
I knew this and everything else. I envied Hammada for what he was: mad, but free. Free to shout, scream and swear, free to piss in the street, free to talk, to say anything and everything.
'Listen, good people – I'm talking to the ones with a maid and *hammam* of their own – look at the misery around you, and shut up. Death never knocks twice – it only comes for the good. The helmets have fallen, good people, and even the sun

sheds tears. . .'

What strange things the man could say! He was our inexhaustible word. Did he even know what he was saying? Mi was rather like him; she would say anything at all.

'Your father used to beat me, my son. . .'

God of the earth, God of heaven, God of hell, help me bear this drone and stay awake to the end. Hammada's voice wrenched me from my thoughts:

'Remember, good people, the locusts and famine – remember the benefits of bread and sugar rationing. It was what you deserved, you murderers. Remember the death of our saint Sidi Ben H'midane, do you remember his lonely death? The tender-hearted ones shed a few wretched tears and everybody went home. . . Remember the poor, remember. . .'

Hammada talked like I pissed, except that he hardly ever stopped. Mi too, but with this difference: she had the certainty of knowing what she was saying.

'He spat in my face, locked me up, abused me in front of other people. . .'

Suddenly I realised I was enormously tired. The muezzin's cry rang out. Mi unfolded her mat mechanically and said her evening prayers. I watched, and was surprised at the speed with which she did her duty to God.

Hammada left me no time to think more about it. His talk was potent: it stopped me thinking.

'. . . to the glory of Allah! Remember despair and fear, remember the helmets, the sheep, and above all the blood. . . In the name of Moulay Brahim, in the name of Abdelkader Jilali, the snow has melted but the grass hasn't pushed up – the roses still aren't budding. Dig up your past, look at your lessons again and bury your stupid women. . .'

The room was brimming with sleep and exhaustion, both stifled by Mi's lamentations. If only she would stop!

'He threatened to repudiate me. I was afraid all the time. He only had to say a word. . .'

I listened to Mi in deep silence. The king of the forest was speaking and tapping his staff on the ground.

37

'Good people, there's no doubt, the women have got your balls – you are only imitation men. Wake up, for God's sake! The birds are up and killing each other – beware of nasty falls. . .'

Dread of filth. Disturbing prophecies. Mi looked at me. I was embarrassed. I guessed her anguish and pretended to give in to the permanent tragedy. She pressed on with the story of her past:

'He threatened to take another wife. When he had plenty of money he used to want two or three. And that was his right. . .'

O my poor mother! So that was the true source of your grief and the real cause of your affliction! Ba Driss would never do anything out of the ordinary. Our religion is great – as great as our insentience and as huge as your desolation. A pause, then Hammada spoke again:

'You go to the mosque, good people, five times a day, when you have to have faith, good people, you have it, you observe Ramadan, you give *zakate*, you make pilgrimages each year to worship at the tomb of Mohammed, you are believers, good Muslims. . .'

Mi touched her brow and kissed her fingertips. Hammada continued:

'Heaven awaits you, good people, it waits – its gates are wide open for you, like Messaouda's legs. . .'

A clear image defined itself in my memory. Mi scowled at me viciously. I pushed my pleasure outside for a breath of air. For a moment I hoped that Mi would see my feet and tell me to wash them. It was night and the light was out. Father would not let us keep the light burning; we were condemned to live in the dark. Without even looking at me, Mi tormented me again with her talking:

'I was a patient and resigned wife. I knew my position depended on my marriage and the number of children I gave him – especially male children. As a repudiated wife I would have been utterly worthless. So I was forced to submit and endure him. . .'

38

She would be wailing for a long time yet. Hammada would ramble on outside, insulting and cursing, perhaps till dawn; then he would go away. Right now he was furious, bursting with invective:

'Hell won't spare you, good people – your deeds are nothing but lies and cant. God can't be fooled by appearances. Good people, in your hearts you hate your neighbours – your blood is black as tar – your hands are dirty and your genitals are filthy. Messaouda isn't your wife – she's the endurance of your piggish greed – leave her be! You only fuck your wives in passing – their vaginas are rusty and spiders spin their webs in them. . .'

Mi looked down and touched her crotch. I felt some disaster was approaching fast. She continued:

'Your pig of a father neglected me; he used to go off all over the place and knew I couldn't do anything about it. Except for some amulets and potions to protect me, I didn't know what I could do to crush him. . .'

My penis was asleep. Mi no longer aroused it: it had grown up. Hammada's words were still gliding into the night:

'By Allah the Omnipotent, the Merciful, by the holy Moulay Driss and the holy Moulay Abdelkader, by the twin breasts of Messaouda, listen to the *fqih*'s song. . .'

I was waiting. Mi got up and I guessed from her walk that she was going to urinate. I took advantage of the interval to shift position and cover my feet. My buttocks were starting to ache. Hammada pursued his frenzy:

'Work, poor tormented man! Work for the sleepers! One by one our doors are closed and our history stays outside where our ancestors left it: a history spun by spiders. . . Our birds have flown, guns in their hands, taking the spades, anguish in their buttonholes, bandoliered with disgust and despair. Our birds have flown good people, our birds have flown. . . but the ones that are left, good people, the ones left – are caged!'

Mi came back and looked for a towel, in vain. She wiped her hands on a corner of her robe, sat down, folded her legs

39

beneath her and fixed me with a long stare. Her eyes had no expression.

'Where was I?'

It was terrible when Mi's memory lapsed. I had to speak, say anything at all to put her back on the track and so justify my presence. I was her touchstone. It must also be said that she did this deliberately to make me speak and let her see if I was taking in what she said.

'I was saying?'

It was obvious. She wanted to make me talk and I did not like talking when I was tired. I managed to open my mouth.

'You. . .'

It was enough to restart the machine.

'Yes, he was a monster. . . And so ridiculous with his great nose and the *tarbouche* he wore to hide his bald head.'

It was promising to be a long night. The teacher had given us multiplication tables to learn by heart. Once again Hammada's voice ripped into the silence.

'Blue bird, white bird, red bird – red as the dead town's blood. . .'

It was frightful when Hammada started singing. Usually I stopped up my ears to block it out, but not that night: Mi was there. She scratched her thigh before continuing.

'As for me, I was good for nothing but washing, polishing, crying, looking after him, producing a child every year, squashing lice, emptying the chamberpots, waiting and waiting again. . .'

There was a sudden salt taste in my mouth. Mi polished, washed, wept, bore a baby each year, killed lice, yes: but I emptied the chamberpots every morning.

Hammada had reached the chorus again in this endless night:

'Blue bird, white bird, red bird – red as blood. . . and the chains of the past. . .'

I glanced furtively at the window; the night was far gone, and my loneliness was vast. I suddenly longed to ask Mi if she knew how many times she had told me her story, changing nothing, omitting nothing. I was not brave enough to interrupt, and she resumed:

'He often brought women back here. Acquaintances or customers, he'd say. He knew I couldn't do anything, couldn't
resist his tyranny in any way. He glutted himself with them
till the early hours. I had to stay up and answer his constant
demands and calls. When he wasn't calling for me, I could
guess what he was doing. He didn't need me any more. . .'

My father was a monster. I realized how much I pitied Mi.
Now Hammada was singing his desperate chorus at the top
of his voice:

'Green bird, green as the grass, red bird, blood-red like the
dead town. . .'

You needed the patience of a rock in our house, with Hammada and Mi. My sleep was wandering, lost, through the cold
streets. I was starting to be truly tired. Hammada suddenly
changed his theme. This is what filtered through to me:

'Winds shall blow. The earth shall shake beneath your feet.
Azraïn will spurn you for he's incorruptible. Unlike all of you.
Then your children will eat your toes and your genitals and
have some peace at last. . .

Blue bird, white bird, green bird, and blood-red. . .

Chains of the present!'

For a moment I wished one of us three would disappear:
Hammada, so he couldn't go on singing his stupid song; Mi,
so she wouldn't exhaust herself any further by her droning;
or me, so I need not put up with either of them any longer.
Hammada was biding his time tonight under our window. He
wouldn't go before the *fqih* had arrived. I pictured him, cram-
med into his *djellaba* like dung in a barrel. Was he hand-in-
glove with Mi? I looked at her secretly: she was now no more
than a dark bulk crouching on the *seddari*. She went on talking
in the same desolate tone:

'He was often dead drunk. One night he undressed, told
me to do the same, and when I was stripped he pissed on me
– the pig. . .'

Like a chamberpot. The smell of urine filled the room. So
Mi's body had been degraded with his filth. What a pig! But

41

then, but then. . . Mi had not put up any resistance, had not rebelled. I knew that. She had got to her feet like a wounded bitch and crept out to wash in the closet. And then wept till dawn. Mi bore the burden of that filth inside herself. But why was she telling me all this tonight? What did she expect from me? Was I worthy of her confidences? Outside, Hammada's monologue went on. He had stopped singing, which was a relief.

'How times change! They have grown harder. The colours used to be clear and it was our work to make them shine. We marched at the head of our fate. We looked for health and were blind with hope: hope for a sunlit future. . . We lived in expectation of Springtime and Liberty: *that* was our destiny. Moulana heard our cry and answered. Then our flowers of hope faded one by one. . . The sun left the sky and all of us helped wipe out the colours. What has become of the promised happiness and prosperity? Didn't the *fqih* foretell all? – "After the storm, always the tempest," he warned and warned again. His very words. Learn them, spread them, feed them! They can brake time. You've been blinded by a dream of freedom, you haven't listened to his words. . .'

Damn! Once Hammada started about the *fqih*, he went on for ever. The night was long and Mi scarcely seemed tired at all. But she yawned once, twice, in her characteristic way, took a sheepskin, got down from the *seddari*, arranged herself comfortably on the ground, crossed her legs beneath her and invoked Allah.

The *fqih* was a strange man, strangely dressed, with a strange voice and expression, a strange life. . . everything about him was strange. He was the dead town's poet, generally known as Kaïss of Azrou. To me he was Moulay Tayab the *fqih*. He never hurt anyone. He came and went. You met him at every street corner. He was always there, inescapable as time (Hammada used to say he was time itself) or an incurable disease. They said he never slept. You might come across him at any hour of the day or night. He never asked anyone for anything and rarely, very rarely spoke. But when he did speak he knew

42

what he was saying: his talk was muddled but astonishing.

Hammada's voice echoed through me:

'Listen, good people, listen to the *fqih*'s story. Hear what happened to him, good people, hear this story, for you abandoned him and no mistake!'

Hammada had definitely decided to spend the night under our window. I would have to put up with it. I stared at the wall in front of me. It was flat and dark. I tried to interrogate it, to decipher something in the old stones, but it was only flat and dark. Mi glanced at me again with dim, red-rimmed eyes. Hammada embarked on the *fqih*'s long and painful story:

'As you know the *fqih* was an extremely good and intelligent man. He was seduced, as you know, by R'qya, the fairest of the fair. They were engaged and. . .'

Mi yawned again and I could see that sleep was locked behind those red eyes, fighting to pull her into the darkness. She could hardly keep up her talking. Exhaustion was starting to win.

'One happy day I almost tried to kill him. He had just taken a second wife. But I was too cowardly. . .'

Unconsciously, Mi must have been asking me to release her from the appalling monster who was maiming her flesh and pride. Was I less cowardly than she? Despair pierced my heart. My mind, half-asleep, ran weird circles around Mi's loneliness. The *fqih*'s story was slipping slowly into the night:

'On their wedding night, good people, the *fqih* was carried off by a *djinn* as you know. Yes good people, make no mistake, by a *djinn* in the middle of the night and taken away to Aïcha Qandischa. . . She married him as you know – and so he made a pact with the devil. . .'

I retched. Mi gave me a withering look and murmured a prayer. I was afraid; so was she. Hammada started again, not giving Mi time even to spit on her tired chest.

'. . . the *fqih* and Qandischa were, as local tradition demands and in humiliation before the *djinnoun*, declared man and wife for bad and for worse. A few days later the fair R'qya died of sorrow and shame as you know. And that's what

43

you've always been told, good people, that's what you've
always been told wherever you go. . . Don't fool with the
devil! After the fair R'qya died the *fqih* became what he is
today: madman and poet. And why? . . .'

Mi's enigmatic gaze was still levelled at me. Her face betrayed nothing beyond a little weariness. This unfinished story
that Hammada was relating in every detail froze me with fear:

'The reason, good people? – Moulay Tayab did not believe
in the *djinnoun*. At night he'd go and taunt them. . .'

For the second time Mi took the chance to spit into the neck
of her *mansouria*. She noticed that I had seen her and I sensed
her embarrassment. In the night and silence Hammada continued, despite my fear and exhaustion:

'He used to cross the river without performing any of the
rituals and never carrying salt. Sometimes he even threw stones
at them. He didn't believe in the *djinnoun*, he swore at them
and pissed in fresh water. . . He went to the graveyard as you
know to sing of his love for R'qya. And one night, good
people, one night. . .'

The wall which had so recently been flat and dark now
stretched away beside the window, stood forward, crouched
back, extended along the opposite side, leaned towards the
ground, straightened up, opened its fiery eye and pinned me
with a terrible gaze. It froze as soon as Hammada opened his
mouth:

'One night Lalla Aïcha heard a suspicious noise and drew
out of the darkness as you know. The *fqih* was pissing peacefully into the river. . .'

A shiver ran up my spine. The wall was already advancing
on me with all the weight of its shadow, obliterating me, grinding me into hideous silence. There was no chance to shout out.
In the street Hammada was telling the *fqih*'s unlikely story to
the stars:

'Aïcha Qandischa was shocked and impressed by the *fqih*'s
audacity and fell in love with him and decided to marry
him. . .'

The wall heaved to its feet again and advanced unsteadily,

44

lurched, narrowly missed a pillar, and waved about so grotesquely that I had a glimpse of its flat, dark rear.

The wall was in front of me, flat and dark. Mi was flat too, as flat as the night that engulfed me, alone. Mi used the pause to get in a few words so that I would not have a moment's rest:

'His new wife was very young – only just thirteen. They said she was very beautiful. He threw her out after nine months because she hadn't produced an heir. . .'

Mi smiled scornfully. Her role of fulfilled mother compensated a little for the role of frustrated wife. Outside the *fqih*'s tale still slid into the turbid night:

'Every night, every night good people, the *fqih* meets his beloved. He meets her every night and every night they resurrect their vast and perfect love. . .'

I could no longer understand anything Hammada said. He must have lost the thread. R'qya was dead, so how could the *fqih* still be meeting her? I looked up and met Mi's eyes. She saw my astonishment. I looked away. She did the same. The wall was still flat, but a little darker now. It was a mystery! I pulled myself together: Hammada was trying to take me in and I had stupidly let myself be tricked for a moment. I knew this story by heart – knew it even better than the others. Hammada continued:

'The people who have seen her swear it's her corpse. R'qya is no more, good people, our beautiful R'qya is dead, peace be to her, Amen!'

Mi feebly touched her forehead and kissed her fingertips. An automatic gesture. I did the same, thinking it would please her. She scowled.

'Hypocrite!' she spat. 'You. . .'

Happily Hammada interrupted just then and gave Mi no time to fly at me.

'It's Qandischa and none other that the *fqih* meets at Titahcen – Qandischa with the goatskin shoes and the heavy chains always dragging behind her. . .'

A great noise suddenly burst in the night. Mi clicked her prayer-beads, and the sound got on my nerves. I could see her lips moving in the dim light. I suddenly felt a great void around me, and began to tremble.

That noise?

That sudden silence?

That strange feeling?

Everyone in Azrou knew the *fqih*'s story. Everyone knew how the weather had broken one night. Black clouds thickened across the clear sky. There was a hailstorm and a violent gale whipped up and flung away all the joy, the smiles and half the trees in Azrou. A furious storm had laid waste all hope of a happy union.

The night was close and cold. I tried vainly to stamp out my growing fear, and started seriously to believe that Hammada had decided to do away with me that night. I looked helplessly up at Mi: her face was now fully shrouded in darkness. I was the victim of Hammada's bitter madness, victim of Mi's haggard past, a victim and a prisoner of the words, exhaustion and sleep that taunted me.

Outside Hammada cleared his throat and spat noisily. The wall before me was flat and dark. Mi yawned and sputtered:

'A rat! What have I ever done to deserve such a beast? God damn the unjust, every one!. . .'

Her mouth could barely bring out the words and they stuck like glue to the dark wall, clinging there with all the strength of their perished sense – their non-sense. Mi was talking to hide her fear:

'He beat me the day I gave birth to our first daughter. He wanted a boy. He claimed I'd never be able to give him a male child and threatened to repudiate me. He didn't look at your sister till three months later – the day he buried her. . .'

Mi spoke haltingly. Was that really to hide her fear, or another trick to keep my attention? I would have to be on my guard; with Mi, you had to be ready for anything. She certainly would not think twice about slapping me across the face, and I was near enough. A bird sang in the night. Hammada began laughing nervously, then swearing blindly. Obscene senseless words flew from his mouth like missiles and ricocheted from

46

the wall, the door, the window, and against my chest.

'Fools – you're fools and everything that happened to me is your fault. Look what you've done to me! You are evil, and more cursed than the devil. I'm a star shining on a cesspool. You are turds and I spit in your ape faces [he spat]. I'm here and I'll always be here watching you and when you're all dead and buried, I'll piss on your graves. . . Just that: piss on them. You give me your bread, you ask me in on Friday, and you hope for my forgiveness – I know all this, Mamma Hajjaja told me one night. No, I'll never forgive you – I'll never pity you because you are pigs stuck in the filth. I'm not asking for anything! Your dry bread, your cold couscous, your rancid butter pancakes and your old faded *djellabas* – I don't want them! I want nothing from you. Keep your hypocrisy and leave me in peace. You can't buy your way to heaven like that. Beware: I'm not as mad as you want to think. It's you who are mad in your hearts and souls. You are all as mad as dogs – mad and depraved. I'll testify on Judgement Day – mad, mad, mad, O children of Aïcha Qandischa!'

Hammada stopped. Mi looked at me questioningly. I turned away and saw the stove. The ashes lay grieving at the bottom. Even the stove was only there to reprove me and serve as final witness when Mi finally hit me. But she wanted to get on with her story:

'Then he deserted us. For three months. Nobody knew where he was. Three months is a long time with two babies and no money. One day they brought him back dead drunk, completely wrecked. Thrown out by the woman he was living with – his money had run out. . .'

Just then the town-crier came by. He must have important news to be allowed to stir the Just from their sleep. This was his lie:

'There is no God but Allah and Mohammed is his Prophet. You shall heed none but the good, *Incha'allah. . .*'

Mi automatically touched her brow and kissed her finger-tips. I did not dare imitate her this time. The crier's ringing words slipped away in the cold night. Mi and Hammada

47

paused to make room for the new words.

'Sid l'Caïd, God give him long life, declares that. . .'

So this was coming to join all the other miseries of speech. Beyond the bitter word that haunted me, I was thinking of death. I had been taken as a very young boy to the cemetery to hear the *tolba* read prayers on my grandfather's tomb. The flood of words from the *tolba*'s withered lungs literally engulfed me. They were curled up on the grey stone, sweating, veins bulging, mouths flecked with spittle. I shut my ears to the verbal assault but in making this pathetic gesture I upset the white bowl they used for sprinkling grandfather's tomb. It smashed into a thousand pieces. A bad omen: it brought down a curse.

Mi was muttering in the dark. She was probably praying. Outside, the dead town rang with new words:

'Jilali Ould Hadda's old grey mule. . .'

Words assaulted me head-on. Father's words had had to be fought first. Later, those of the *m'sid* and the school; then Mi's; then Hammada's and the *fqih*'s. Finally the whole world's words at once.

I foundered in the chaos of words and did not know why they had destructive power over me. Perhaps because the monstrous importance that language had for us – and against us – split my memory. It had started with insults and nagging and continued with the uplifting story of Mamma Ghoula. After that I was entirely at the mercy of the unquestionable word.

A pause, then the crier raised his voice again:

'. . . has just been delivered of a hinny at the *fondouq*. He reminds you – and God bless him for it – that it's an omen of the end of time. He says further – and God grant him long life for it – that you must ponder this, and crave His Mercy. . .'

I was crushed under this avalanche of words which marked the boundaries of my cliff-hanging universe. Black language still slipped into my childish memory and left its trace. I was used to bad news but not on this scale. 'So soon!' I thought. 'O God, why? I haven't seen anything yet. . .'

Mi's lips briefly stopped moving. She invoked Allah before

stealing a glance at the closed window. We were waiting for the rest of the news, and it came soon enough:

'He makes it known to you at last, and God give him long life for it, that after the Friday prayer we will leave the Latif together. Everybody must come to the mosque. There is no God but Allah and Mohammed is his Prophet – heed only the good, *Incha'allah*. . .'

The crier went farther off, leaving me in a terrible state. The rest must have been peacefully sleeping the sleep of fools. They were not worthy of Mi's confidences, nor grown-up enough to listen to the street noises.

As soon as the crier had gone Hammada carried on his lunacy exactly where he had left off. Perhaps what had just been said had no interest for him. He was a madman, on the margin of society.

'My father had seven brats. I was the eighth. My mother was twenty-three and racked with pains in her womb. My father raped her every night and she was pregnant every year. Eight brats in eight years of marriage. A hard bed, hard bread, hard life, and exile thrown over the past. Messaouda the strange strained expression, scar of time, her sex gaping, the useless sperm, her cunt putting the grown-ups to sleep, the milky sperm. . . O where are you my scorched dove? *T'fou! khzit!* Aïcha Qandischa curses you. With her goatskin shoes and her heavy chains, she rapes you all in the person of the *fqih*. You hang your heads, you gang of cowards! You burned incense, you all prayed together, and you forgot – you begged your saints to keep you from calamity, then went home as if nothing was wrong, and me, I took out my *sebsi* and smoked all the miseries of time. Allah sees us, Allah watches over us. But for protection. Allah is great, Allah is mighty, Allah. . . Allah. . .

Open your thighs
to ease and slide
draw me inside
zib. . . *zib*. . .'

49

Hammada fell silent. Mi was embarrassed; she blushed and looked at the ground. I stared at her. She sighed and awkwardly stroked the bellows. Her eyes misted. Her mouth sagged and gaped. I touched my penis: it was fast asleep. The night outside was plunged in a suspicious silence. What was Hammada doing? Could he have gone without saying goodnight? In the quiet of the night I made out a familiar sound, and guessed the reason for the silence.

Hammada was busy. Just for a moment, I was not afraid. Hammada spurted. I heard it very clearly – as did Mi, for she looked round at me. I could not bear her tired gaze. Her questioning expression spoke her thought unmistakably. She was leaning forward a little and her face was no longer in darkness. Slightly annoyed now, I looked at her and all the scars of time on her faded face were there to read. Life!

That second I thought I saw a glimmer in her eyes, and was astonished: a kind of frightful joy flushed through me. She moved heavily back and her face was shrouded again in shadow. Nothing to stare at now; my thoughts wandered.

Mi was the youngest girl in a family of six children: four girls and two boys. Her father gave her a man on her fourteenth birthday. The man became my father. After long negotiations the two men agreed the size of the dowry, the preparations and the date for the wedding. One evening, grandfather – God forgive him! – announced the good news to the family. Grandmother wailed. Mi said nothing: she had nothing to say. She had the blessings of God and her parents. Anyway, grandmother had always taught her man's incomparable value as well as woman's need to be a wife and mother. She beat her often so she could learn submission and accept humiliation.

Grandfather was happy: this arrangement completed his paternal duties. He had done what he had to do: unearthed a good husband for his daughter. The great hope had been realized – and it was one less mouth to feed.

Some time after the wedding she came home to spend the day with her parents. She had argued with Father. Grandfather came in from the fields in a black rage. He took Mi into a separate room and tore into her:

'Pull yourself together! There's no place for you here, or for anyone else who is married. Your place is with your husband. You're behaving like a little girl. At the moment he could very well repudiate you: it is *you* who is in the wrong. You've abandoned the marriage bed. What will people say? Where would you go? You mustn't leave your house whatever happens. You say he hit you – what's wrong with that? He's completely within his rights. He's your husband, isn't he? God preserve him for you! Go home and behave like a wife, if you don't want to come to grief. Above all, don't set foot here again if you are angry with him. Stay at home. Time will sort everything out. Time always sorts things out. You will be a mother in no time and you'll understand. And he'll understand too. You're fed, you have a roof over your head – what more do you want? Go! Thank God for heaping his blessings on you. Go and beg your husband's forgivness and promise me never to do this again. It's wrong – it's madness to behave like this. Go, my daughter, and remember that from now on your place is by your own hearth. I've done all I could. Now you depend completely on your husband and must obey him in everything. Understand that I have no rights over you. Go home, my daughter and may Allah protect your household!. . .'

Mi picked up her bundle and went home, giddy at the prospect of climbing back down to her humiliation. She realized this marked the end of her life. She finally submitted to her husband and resigned herself to her new existence.

Hammada gave a rattling gasp. The reprieve had just ended. I sank back into a state of dreadful turmoil. He started singing an absurd little song:

O my salted grasshopper
where do you wander?
– In the garden of delights
– What have you drunk, what eaten there?
– Apples and scents,

O *qadi*, keeper of the
mysteries' key!

During the silent intervals I listened to Mi's laboured brea-
thing. Anguish swelled in me, crushing my loneliness. I felt
insignificant in the face of such violence. Grandmother always
said that a frightened camel will never graze at ease. I was a
camel which never lived in peace. I looked sidelong at the wall
and could not see anything at all. It had become invisible. It
loved to take me by surprise in my white fear. It fooled about
like a brat, waited patiently, and at the chosen moment, surged
out of my anguish and rejoiced in taking every nightmare
shape. It was aggressive and I was unarmed. I did not look at
it directly; I was somehow embarrassed in front of it.

Now the shadow separated us. I could hardly make out her
hands resting on the sheepskin, and had no wish to imagine
them. Mi blew her nose loudly before continuing her stale
story:

'Then you arrived – you arrived. . .'

A thunderclap stopped me hearing the rest. In the shadows
I guessed what she was saying: that I was a boy, as she had
hoped; that Father had sworn to repudiate her if she had produced a girl. Now Father could hold nothing against her, now
he need fear no more for his virility – this was the proof for
all to see. There I was: man and heir. Honour was spared, the
inheritance safe, and his smile restored.

'And Hafid?'

The question stuck in my throat. Mi spoke quickly. I knew
she was unloading, getting rid of everything; then she would
stop talking and go to sleep. Freedom was almost in sight.
Suddenly I was very nervous and more deeply despairing than
ever before. I looked at her shadowed face: her eyes were
looking sharply back at me. I looked down.

Although she was small, Mi had been beautiful in her youth.
I knew that: she told me so. Father reduced her to a caricature
of woman. Father, time, and fate. I wanted to get up, kiss her
hands, and tell that I loved her in spite of all her wrinkles and

griefs, and in spite of time. . . that I loved her above all *for* her wrinkles and grief. Cold and exhaustion paralysed me where I sat.

Outside Hammada coughed, cleared his throat once more, beat his stick on the hard ground, and set off on his monologue:

'The birds are hungry, the birds are thirsty, the birds are afraid. They are dying – the dried-up sea at the stream's mouth. Despair swells the sky with hate and misery. Sleep is seized at the eyelids' tips and tears are stopped too. Life is there in its leaden uniform – and a sorrowing people defeated by fear. History waits for no one. The bloody earth is ready for seeding. Song is a rock for breaking, a stone to hurl at destiny, a stone to build with. . . My body, I want you to be a sign, spurning dreams and promises – I wish you courage for the future, and freedom. . .'

I was appalled at Hammada's speeches; the words made no sense. Where could he have found them? I told myself there would be no sleep that night. Listening to those words and thinking about them, I realized that I had them, all of them, inside me: simple words, impoverished words, stripped and shorn words. I absorbed them and repeated them to myself.

There was nobody left in the street. We had reached the early hours and all the lights were out. I could feel Mi's heavy stare. I turned briskly aside and concentrated on the flat, dark wall. A black spider was crawling up it. Mi's silence unnerved me. She picked her lower lip in a familiar manner; she used to pick at her lip like that whenever she did not have anything in particular to say or when she could not find the words for what was in her head. She carried on in the same desolate voice as before:

'You are the family's pride, and my own pride. You let me forget my unhappiness and my own condition. I trust you. You're a man now. You can do much if you want to. You can. . .'

She said this in the same way she might have asked me to fetch her something to drink. Flat, vacant words. Exhaustion.

All I remember is this: she was weeping in her usual silence. Outside, Hammada's voice jabbered in the night. Still black: no sign of dawn. I was worn out. A strange, pregnant silence suddenly spread inside and out. It was all beyond me; was this journey's end, the end of torture? I was just getting used to the quiet when a dog started barking. Hammada spat on the ground and beat it with his stick. And the noise rang in my memory.

'Go away!' he shouted. 'Go away, filthy animal, foul creature!. . .'

There was a loud noise and the dog gave an almost human yelp. It dragged itself off whimpering into the darkness. For a long time I could hear its howls scraping the night's silence. Crouching uncomfortably, baring his bad teeth to the night, Hammada began swearing at the dog. I was ashamed and timidly lowered my eyes from Mi. Hammada laughed his dusty laughter. Like his laughter and gestures, the man's words horrified me. Everything about him horrified me. He could not sit still outside. Mi was talking while I kept watch. I pressed on alone towards the coming dawn: only a few minutes' suffering and uncertainty, no more.

I had created a world of my own during this endless night: a world of tiny sounds, brief silences and nostalgic words. Someone coughed outside. It wasn't Hammada. Whoever it was coughed in an almost human way. Steps approached the house and stopped very near our window. And at the same moment rain struck the town with hurricane force. As if the sky had split. The rain fell like a fist, thick and savage, sparing neither houses nor trees, neither Hammada nor the newcomer, neither my loneliness and fear nor Mi's exhaustion and despair. For a minute our roof tried to resist, then the water came through. The rain lasted as long as it took to wash our furious words away. I said a few hurried prayers that I had learned at the *m'sid*. I was scared; Mi too. I thought the end of the world had come.

Hammada spat, swore, beat the streaming ground with his stick, rolled in the water, tore his hair, sobbed. Mi swallowed

54

and clucked unpleasantly. She looked at me. Lightning blazed the room and right there before me was a mysterious face. Outside, the rain still scourged the town and some of its consciences. Hammada was in complete despair and the wall was wrestling with its own shadows. It finished up prostrated, beaten, panting hard. Explosions of thunder shook the building. Hammada swore. Mi raised her eyes to the heavens and her gaze dashed against the roof. She stammered a prayer and clicked her beads. Hammada struck the wall with his stick and the blows rang in my soul. Pain appeared on the flat, dark wall, Mi's whispers filled the room and flayed my ears. If R'qya had lived, if the animal had behaved like a man to Mi, if she had been a rebellious woman towards him, if. . . – none of this would have happened!

The rain stopped as abruptly as it had begun. Mi's stutterings stopped too, as did the click of the beads. Hammada spat and threw a final insult after the storm:

'I am the night. . .'

Silence – the deepest silence – absorbed his words. I never understood anything the *fqih* said. Tonight, as so many nights, I was forced to hear him out and keep my wound to myself.

'I am the dessicated night. . .'

He did not need to insist: we knew it already. His words were going to travel through time and space to shatter against my memory.

'. . . I am fate's shadow
the quivering hour
of last judgement'

Hammada was quiet at last. Mi was listening closely to the newcomer, and I guessed this gave her bitter comfort.

At the start of his career as lunatic and poet, the *fqih* used to hide away in the darkest corners: he didn't like his meditations being disturbed. Alerted by a local boy, we converged on him, surrounded him and made him invent poetry or tell us about his boyhood.

'We lived in Casablanca,' he told us one day. 'In a white house in the Ben M'sik. I was fifteen and full of guilt. During the day I went to school. In the evenings I went with my shoe-box round the better districts looking for dusty shoes. I was old enough, and had to pay for my board at home. Father called it my "contribution". There was no room for idlers in our house. Father worked in the fields: he was a *khammass* and was paid a fiftieth of his master's profits. One night. . .'

Mi was slipping little by little nearer the brink of sleep but refused to yield freely. I watched her; she was half in shadow. Her fingers flicked her prayer beads very fast. The *fqih*'s voice rose up:

'What is this moaning wind
What is this voice that calls me
And what is this strange passion
Around and strangling me?'

The *fqih*'s poetry made my head spin with its incoherence and obscurity. So meaningless. 'Lunatics' poetry,' as Father used to say. He leaped from subject to subject with bewildering speed. Was it really poetry or just an aberration? I did not know at all, and was more interested in his life story:

'I remember – Mina was crying. There was blood on the ground and on her legs. I couldn't understand what was happening to me. Unbearable sorrow, and my father beating me. I was bleeding all over. It was raining. My mother, brothers and sisters were howling in the cold night. My aunt hugged her daughter to her breast and cursed me. I could not feel the blows any more. Sleep, cold, and blood. Sorrow was all of me: I was nothing but sorrow. Mina was shaking. My father dragged me through the mud by my hair. Everyone in the quarter rushed up one after another and spat on me and cursed me. I remember sorrow, night, cold, sleep and blood. . .'

The events tripped and shoved in his tired memory.

'. . . Night. Always night-time bringing me the same old torture in her old robes, torture that only stopped at daybreak.

56

My six brothers and sisters slept packed in a row. Mother waited while Father drank his tea and quietly smoked the *kif* that he'd carefully prepared in the afternoon. I hutched down in my corner and slept with my eyes open. I remember the cold, sleep, exhaustion. . .'

I felt a violent spasm in my stomach. Under our window the *fqih* was juggling with his misshapen poetry:

'Silence murmurs in the high sails of oblivion
And fear unfolds its vulture's wings into infinity
A little corner of boiling wind
Autumnal fire burns away
Faces that never laugh or smile
Faces of the resurrected
And the dead on parole. . .'

The new words slipped into the night and escaped my groping mind. Their bare meaning was only a pretext. Everything about the words was absurd. The chanting stopped for a moment, giving way to the voice of silence. It was as if those shabby words were waiting for a miraculous breath of life. The room's settled silence enveloped me. Mi was listening with barely-opened eyes to this ghostly voice sent by Providence, with the storm, to keep me in exile. Mi started to mumble, finding her words only with difficulty, and Hammada had nothing more to add.

The *fqih* stopped talking. Bouchahda winked at us. We were getting impatient. The *fqih* took a bit of rag from his pocket and spat into it. He put his 'handkerchief' back and continued his story; it was time.

'There was no light in our hole for me to do my homework. Like everyone else in the Ben M'sik, my father thought one five-centime candle a night was quite enough. Mother used to stick it on a spike set into the door. Each night my six brothers and sisters fought over the pictures in my old school book. How tolerant my teacher was! He often told me to take more care of my things and I never dared tell him I often found my mother poking the fire with my pen. To her, it was just a bit of wood that did to poke the fire.' No one ever dared to interrupt the *fqih*. His talk always left us feeling disgusted and in the end we adopted the violence of his words ourselves.

Before they accused him of madness the *fqih* had been a very ordinary man. The poor devil soon took advantage of the specious indulgence that was extended to all who escaped from the straight line of time. Everyone in Azrou knew the circumstances of his fall, which is why he was more feared than respected. His hoarse voice jerked me out of thought:

'Oblivion hacks her tomb
in memory's room
with despairing hands
burying her memories
of life's shifting uncertainty
in despair
and in disgust. . .'

The archaic lines spun out to my ears. The clay-coloured words grated in the *fqih*'s mouth. They collided in the dark as they spawned in the depths of my being and scattered in my broken mind. A blue dream coasted into my soul and broke up on my weariness. I tugged the blanket over my bare feet. Mi glanced up with vague eyes. I was sorry I had moved at all. The flat, dark wall still taunted me.

Twelve of us made a ring round the *fqih* and listened to his story:

'Night. Always night. A harsh test for a frail conscience. Now and then I got out of our foul den before dawn and set off to school, to check my lessons under a street-lamp. It did not take Father long to find me and drag me back to the pit, grumbling at me to get back home and stop making trouble, as vermin like me could only become porters in the docks, shoe-blacks, *khammass*, or shepherds. "Studying is for people with money. Where have *you* seen an old dog learn new tricks? You'll do better learning a trade – as it is you have stronger knees than me. Get home!"

'Night! As soon as its black cloak spread over the town, we

gobbled our supper and off to bed. Father smoked a last *sebsi*.
Mother undid her black belt and bent over the seven close-
packed shadows to make sure we hadn't died of hunger or
cold. . .'

At first Moulay Tayab knew no one in Azrou. He worked
and slept at the bakery. Then Moulay Kaddour suggested
working at the cinema. In the morning he put up posters in
the square, and in the evening he kept an eye on things. Sometimes he even took the money, and Hassan the projectionist
taught him how to load the reels. Moulay Tayab went around
the town before each performance carrying a great board
covered on both sides with little posters. We were his escort
and he repeated his raucous cry in every street:

'At the cin'ma – 'merican film wit Gary Cooper at nine-
thirty, whoever's listening! Nothing but fighting in this film,
and the hero isn't killed at the end – I repeat, the hero is NOT
killed at the end of the film. At the cin'ma – 'merican film. . .'

Mi was gradually slipping towards sleep. She had stopped
talking; that was the important thing. The whining voice still
ruined the silence:

'Dogs we are, in search
of a smile
silent bodies
wandering in time, lost,
hunting for a rotting corpse
to keep us alive
avoiding worms
and all changes. . .'

Suddenly I was shaken by these useless words, still pouring
relentlessly down the steep slope of the *fqih*'s mind with amaz-
ing fluency, and with total indifference to my exhaustion.
These lines were so tired that they died even in mid-flight
towards me. Hammada had stopped beating the ground with
his stick. He was no longer shouting, talking or moving. He
felt so small beside the *fqih* that he did not dare show so much
as his rotten teeth.

Still attentive, we followed the next stage of the *fqih*'s story:

'My mother climbed on to the bed and waited. My father said his prayer and joined her as quickly as he could. As soon as the candle had gone out, making the place unbelievably dark, the shadows fired my dismal imagination. The bed very soon began its noises. My father coughed and flailed about and grunted. Nothing was more maddening than father's grunting and it woke me every night. Then my eyes got used to the dark and I saw my mother's body dimly moving at the end of the bed, up against the wall. If only I could have been struck deaf so as not to hear my father's gasps! O if only I could!. . . Didn't my brothers and sisters hear anything at all? Why didn't they wake up so we could fight those sleep-stopping movements together? Why did I have to bear that agony alone? Why? Why? Why?'

Suddenly the wall sat up straight and Mi spat into her *mansouria*. She did that whenever she was afraid – it was a way to fend off evil. Hammada was silent. The *fqih* had relieved him in this, the longest night. Mi, the wall, Hammada, and now the *fqih*. I must be going crazy at last. A few solitary lines came in and lodged at the base of my skull:

'I come to you with white words
filling my voice
and songs unravished
I come to seize you in your absence
and lead you towards the sun'

A song? A poem? I discovered a new dimension of words as I advanced across the *fqih*'s voice: words carved out of silence and hesitation, unforeseen reactions, melody and superfluity. Meaning crept away behind infinite naïvety, and I enjoyed feeling the tenderness and violence of words on my skin. I identified with the *fqih*'s lunacy in the hope of finding my own voice.

Mi was fond of the two tramps under our window. She had even learned a few of the *fqih*'s chants, and I surprised her several times singing them in the kitchen. The first time I tried to drive them away, Mi attacked me for my disrespect:

'What have they done to you, boy? You can't leave them alone! They never hurt a fly. You and your friends have already throttled the cat. You killed the hens with your catapults and blinded the neighbours' dog in one eye. And the monkey. . .'

She stopped. She did not dare list any more of my crimes. What had been done to the monkey was done mainly for her. That one was not my fault: I thought I had done it for the best.

'Get out!' she said. 'You are wicked. What have I done to deserve a son like you? . . .'

After that the two vagabonds who would not hurt a fly regularly spent the night under our window.

Sometimes Moulay Tayab stopped and said he would finish his story another day. He'd pretend to be tired, or say he was falling asleep. Then Bouchahda filled his *sebsi* with *kif*, lit it and offered it to him. The *fqih* accepted with a smile and made himself comfortable, smoking quietly, before picking up the tale:

'I used to wonder: Do all my friends at school sleep with their fathers' gasping in their ears and the bed creaking and their mothers writhing against the wall?'

And these events unfolded again in Moulay Tayab's memory. He hurried on:

'It rained all night. The wind blew and we had a tasty supper. My father had brought a whole pound of tripe. My aunt stayed after the meal, waiting for the rain to stop before going home to the other side of the quarter. "As long as mother keeps her and her daughter here," I thought, "we'll have their breath added to our own and be able to stay warm." We didn't have a fire and there were not enough blankets to go round. . .'

There was a pause in which I gauged with horror the sheer distance separating me from the words. I could no longer see Mi at all, and my trembling body was being caressed by new words:

'How many of us suffering
in the white night of our exile
How many of us dying
shadowed by a bastard history
How many of our corpses
beaten by fear of times past
ringed with fine promises
and scattered dreams
What is our strength?
How many our voices?'

I did not understand the *fqih*'s poetry. Was it all simply idiotic? My stomach churned; I felt sick. The wall broke into a grotesque dance, raising one foot and almost falling on my head. The idea of having to leave part of myself on the cold ground that night was appalling. I controlled myself as best I could but finally surrendered to my sad fate and vomited up all my child's despair. In a flash my hatred was spreading before me in a foul pool that caught the passing words and trapped them stickily. In the darkness Mi touched her face and changed position once again. She had stopped turning round and I was alone with my failure and despair.

Just after midnight, Moulay Tayab got up to piss against the wall. We waited impatiently for him to resume his story. He loved keeping us in suspense. He returned, but could not be made to talk; he settled down in his corner and got ready to sleep.

'Son of a whore!' shouted Bouchahda. 'Your prattle doesn't come cheap, does it? If you ever do that again we'll bugger you one by one and tell the whole town you have been buggered, and then you'll look silly, you shit!'

The *fqih* did not budge – scarcely deigned to glance at Bouchahda, who took out his *sebsi* for the third time and filled it with *kif* for Moulay Tayab. Who did not take it. Bouchahda squatted down beside him and grabbed his collar.

'If you don't smoke this *sebsi* I'll stick it up your arse. I haven't gone to all this trouble for nothing and we have all decided to stay and hear your story to the end. So don't fool with us. You bastard! I know you want this pipe – so take it and let us save our breath. . .'

Moulay Tayab reached out and, forcing a laugh, took the pipe. He put it down and carried on his story. We closed in around him.

'The candle had burned right down. "My aunt must be deaf!" No, she was snoring, which was why she did not hear my father whinnying or the noise of my mother wedged at the end of the bed. Then the storm broke. The hammering rain drowned every other sound. Rain and cold. A winter's night. I was shaking like a leaf. I wanted to squeeze closer to my brothers and sisters for warmth, closer to my aunt, closer to my cousin. My cousin! – I had completely forgotten her. In the darkness I couldn't quite remember what she looked like. What if I went and looked at her face close up? I could creep over with no risk of being heard as long as the old bed was grinding and my aunt snoring.

And the film of those events snapped in the *fqih*'s mind.

Outside the words slipped into the night and shattered the silence around my solitude. The *fqih* stopped for a moment and my exhaustion closed down like fog. The poet coughed feebly in the dark. Then, lowering his voice, he pursued his dream:

'The age of the *harka* is over
Life isn't folklore
Burnt-out dreams
And mouldy promises
Raise the dead
And carry off our corpses. . .'

Mi had not spoken for a long time. Hammada likewise, and all the other street noises. Night walked over my exhaustion in velvet shoes. As a sacrificial child I would be spared none of the torture. From now on I had to face the cruelty of the word alone.

I wondered if the story the *fqih* was in the middle of telling us that night was not just his own invention. I knew he was a liar, and a shameless one: he would tell any story for a twist of *kif*. He would have made an excellent public storyteller. Like everyone else, I listened to him. We were all alike when it came to pestering somebody. The *fqih* peered feverishly about him before continuing:

'I was struggling behind my father in the police station. I couldn't understand what was happening to me. Pain, yes. . . There I was. . . Pain! I was terribly sick – my back – that was it. . . Pain, and blood on my sister's thin legs. I had got the wrong body. Mina was trembling. She wasn't crying any more. That was it. . . Pain, blood, and the night. Mother's screams and Father's deafening shouts filled the house. He beat me and dragged me by the hair for a long time through the mud, swearing at me, scratching me, drawing blood with his bites. . .

"Lock him up!" he yelled hysterically. "Treat him like a convict. This bastard isn't my son! The pervert! Lock him up – lock him up – kill him!. . ."'

Someone passed by outside, greeted the *fqih*, and vanished into the night. There was a noise in the street. Mi jumped up. Our neighbour had just taken out her slop bucket. Hammada growled, 'Hmph, bless this day!' and was silent. The awakening noises left no room for doubt: dawn was breaking. I was no longer alone, and the town was slowly emerging from the shadows. The muezzin called for the first prayer. This really was the end. A grey morning rose over the town. Mi twitched in her sleep. I looked out at the new day being born before I fell asleep too. I had no strength left to sustain my lone voyage across the exhaustion of words and the madness of sleep.

Farther off, there was silence.

O Azrou, king of rock! Your
cedars plunge their roots in arid
soil which nothing waters. They
turn your blood of snow into
green leaves and all Morocco rejoices. . .
                                        —M. A. Lahbabi

Hafid woke me next morning, looking for his marbles under
my mattress. Mi had gone. The sheepskin lay on the ground.
The bands Mi wore to hold up the sleeves of her *mansouria*
were on the little bench. It was ten o'clock: too late for school.
There would be no teacher's stick whipping round my drowsy
head today. I would certainly be beaten tomorrow but at least
this morning there would be no bullying from our master.

My absence would be a disappointment to Monsieur Marin. I
did not understand it at all. He said I was a brilliant pupil,
yet he hardly ever spared me his imaginative punishments. I
thought:

'This morning your cane won't sting my dirty servile feet.
You won't ask which dish I'd prefer and I won't answer: bread
and butter, or couscous, or chicken, or. . . . I shan't watch you
open your cupboard and choose the exact stick to match the
meal, and Thami won't hold my feet steady. I won't have to
wear the dunce's cap. My spindly back won't shake under the
weight of your old stick and I won't clamp your rusty bit in
my mouth. I won't grit my teeth and scrape my hands on the
playground gravel. Won't listen to your laughter shattering
the silence and won't have to hold back my tears. . .'

I did not want to think about the next day. I had a plan:
after the last Arabic lesson I'd go to the *fondouq* and wash my

hands in horse urine. Or I could rub them with garlic. That smelt really bad when there were forty reeking pairs of hands in a small classroom. We used these two ploys to make the pain pass more quickly.

I am always surprised when people talk about the 'good old days' and recall their happy years at school. There is no such thing as a happy school. If you are honest, the 'good old days' were mere hell.

At school we were beaten more than we were taught: flogging first and foremost, and flogging ever after. And it was only afterwards that we were taught anything – which is to say, nothing much at all. The nazarenes (Christians) were there not to take our training and education in hand, but to make sure we knew how little and useless we were. They obliterated us, slaughtered us, in the name of their own intelligence, superiority and strength, and in the name of an incomprehensible, simply alien civilization. It was a massacre!

For their part, our parents were scarcely interested in our education. They never knew what we were doing at school, whether we attended as we ought or worked well in class. They only became a bit concerned when it was too late and there was nothing to be done. Our existence passed unseen. We were there, like our mother or the *kanoune*, which had often burned out.

Mi's return solaced me a little. She brought in my glass of tea and some barley bread. While she was making me comfortable I asked her a question:

'Mother, how did people get the idea of building their houses on a mountain side?'

It was only an excuse to break the silence lying on the room. She answered by quoting the Koran, and tiptoed out:

'He who created heaven and earth in the true creation, the day he said "Be!", and it was.'

And Azrou was the eternal rocky misery of men. Azrou was born of stone as a sign of time and was encrusted for ever in its people's sight. It was a defiance of time in the midst of mountains and forests of oak and cedar. It was the icy coldness of long winter nights and the impossible heat of burning summer days.

Azrou was ash at the bottom of an old clay stove, expertly moulded in a style so ordinary that it even included the roads linking the traditionally fierce north to the empty south, and the powdered swollen east to the desperately slumbering west. The whole package in its original décor with its own natural beauty, all exported free in tourists' cameras.

All life begins on these roads – simple and touching, or occasionally brutal and lawless. When you set out on one of these roads for the first time, you are on course for a much wider exploration than you think. These mystic highways do not lead only to Agadir, Tinghir, or Rissani, but towards an alien, sacred universe where you will grasp the mystery of an existence at once pure and terrifying.

Once out of the rut of Azrou, you will see a truth: you are happy. You are an ambassador and pilgrim, questing for the absolute in a landscape whose originality and multiple contrasts are already erasing you. The blasting wind, the burning sun, the soaring mountains, the yielding snow, the *chergui* scrawling its mark on time, the unknown man sighing and groaning, the holy void raving, the sky spreading across the horizon, the nights fleeing, the sealing waves and time stopping. . . You discover a new harmony there. You become savage again. *Life* is there.

If you climb to the top of one of the mountains overlooking the town, you will easily see the simplicity that draws people and nature together. You can see the entire town from there: small as the bruised hearts of its people, solid as Hammada, hard as Akechmir, patient as Messaouda – whom you will eventually rediscover at the end of this prostituted, silent land. 'Azrou the widow!' as the *fqih* liked to call her.

There is neither a real 'town' nor a *medina* at Azrou. There is just Azrou, nothing more. Simply Azrou. The town's quarters are neatly separated from each other by the fated boundaries ordained by nature. Children were sworn, eternal enemies. Each district had its own gang, its own hill, its own football team and its own laws.

The games we played against the teams from other quarters always ended in a bloody fight. The beaten team wanted revenge and we spent entire days on the big field, converted into a football pitch for special matches. The friendly matches we played once in one district and the return fixture in the other. The referee was invited from a neutral quarter. He was ignored, and told off if he tried to cheat or get away before the end of the game – which could last from morning till night. We used to stop when we couldn't tell the ball from the player's foot. We promised to get together and finish the proceedings another day and parted on good terms, throwing punches or stones at one another.

Each gang was known by the name of its quarter. There were the sons of Ahadaf, the sons of Tizi, the sons of Bouiglial and the Kechla, and it was unwise for anyone to venture alone into another quarter. The sons of Ahadaf did not have Turkish baths in their quarter, and never dared go to the baths in the Kechla without their parents. Even then they had to be careful.

When we came across one another out of our respective quarters – at Tanoute, for example, where we learned to swim – we never played together. Each played with his own group and a fight usually broke out immediately and a battle gradually developed, with everyone defending his rights and honour with fists, nails and stones.

Each season had its own game. When it rained we had chases down the muddy streets of the quarter, rallies under the shop awnings, bird-hunting expeditions, or 'three dinifri', adapted from the French hide-and-seek. When it snowed we went sledging on bread-boards (transformed into toboggans for the occasion), and spent evenings around the fire listening to Mamma Ghoula's interminable tales.

In spring we played with marbles, hoops, *kâabs*, spinning-tops, or *tiqoulla*. Our favourites in summer were little go-carts made of planks and ball-bearings stolen from scrap merchants.

Sometimes we went fishing. And when it was really hot, we went swimming at Titahcen or Tanoute.

We filled our days as best we could. Life was not easy in the emotional desert which our parents constantly strove to make even more arid. They had no time for our games. To them we were always men, and had to show ourselves worthy of the very privilege that stripped us of our childhood; so we played in secret.

On Tuesdays we looked at Azrou, its *douars* and *zaouyas*, with new eyes – the eyes of the outsiders, riding donkeys and mules, who packed our streets, baths, cafés, houses and everywhere else. We spent hours on a hill overlooking the *fondouq*, excitedly watching the animals mount each other while their masters were about their business.

The outsiders looked frank and naïve as they inspected Azrou, and it delighted us to know we were more educated, civilized and observant than them. We even played naughty tricks on them – stole their things and misdirected them.

'The *hammam*, my son?'

'Go straight ahead, sir, turn left, up the steps, then right, five hundred meters on and the baths are at the end of the street. . .'

'Thank you, my son. God bless you!'

The baths were two steps behind him.

Or again:

'The bus for Timahdit, my son?'

'I'll show you the way, sir. . .'

And the poor *Chleuh* would find himself at the Moulay Kaddour cinema (a disgusting fleapit). He settled down in a rusty seat, watched strange scenery rush past, and thought at the end of the film he was at Timahdit.

It was a game, one way of passing the time in a tiny town where life seemed to hang from the hands of an old clock, turning in pursuit of time – which was always too fast for it.

And then Azrou, taken away in others' eyes. At sunset the

outsiders went home, men and goods together on the animals' backs, the women following obediently on foot.

I did not go to the *fondouq* for horse urine after the last Arabic lesson. A fight broke out at the door between our leader and Brik Azzi. Exercise books and *djellabas* were thrown down. The kids ringed the two enemies, who faced each other and waited for the signal. A misunderstanding, which had been carefully fostered during the lesson, had started it.

'Don't be scared,' they said to Brik Azzi. 'You'll show him! Don't worry, you are stronger than he is. He told us himself he's frightened of you. Don't forget to say a prayer before the fight.' Then, among themselves:

'Azzi's really gone mad. Who would dare have a go at the bravest and strongest one in the quarter? There will be blood – this will be good!'

Akka had been our unchallenged leader since he beat T'hami. He was fearless and valiant and we obeyed him blindly. He took all the decisions, picked the members of the gang, organized the 'tournaments', collected the dues, kept the accounts, even laid his life on the line to defend the honour of the quarter. . . We obeyed and paid homage with marbles and oranges. We kept close to him and hoped he would be kind and protect us. That was the set-up in every quarter.

A boy came forward and tossed a stone into the middle of the ring. Akka seized it, spat on it and lobbed it to Brik, who picked it up in turn, spat on it, and threw it back at the feet of his enemy. The fight began amid yelling and cheering.

The winner would become our invincible captain and his voice would be our oracle of wisdom and truth. His foe would slink back into the crowd and everything would return to normal until the next confrontation.

The ancient gramophone in the public café played one of Mohamed Abdeluahab's old songs all day long. We could not

70

understand why they liked the Egyptian singer. We were not allowed inside the café but that didn't stop us lending a hand now and then, when there was a bloody argument between grown-ups after a game of belote or *ronda*, or *aïta*. Père Haddou the proprietor was keen to sell us his famous *kif* under the counter, and we smoked it outside the town. We chewed mint afterwards to cover the smell.

The café was as important a place as the *fondouq*, the oven, the *m'sid* or the *hammam*. Azrou would have been no more than a common *douar* if it had not had those everyday necessities. We were town-dwellers, and never missed a chance to remind outsiders of the fact.

We also mischievously loved listening to the French army veterans, talking 'French':

'Me, I went to France in '40. Ah, France! I saw Montpilyer, Morseille, Paritz – ah, Paritz! A huge town, so many people, and cars, and beesickles. Ah, Paritz! Ah!. . .'

'You shut up about France, you! I was Italian during the war. I went to Milana, Romeo, Vanish. . . the Italians and the Moroccans were like brothers. War over, Italians give me presents. I leaving, friends crying. . .'

'Hey! Hey! I was in Indochina. . . I knew it like my hand back. You, still the size of little finger. One day I was fed up. The captin shouts, I say shit to him and punch him in the mouth. . .'

The street was much more important than the café. It captivated us as soon as we could walk. We became its children and spent most of our time in it. It knew us better than our parents did, and each stone, each corner, each shop, each handful of dirt had a mystic significance for us. A thousand emotional ties bound us to it: we knew one another inside out and we loved each other. The street was part of our childhood just as we were part of its history.

No matter how far back I look in my memories, I can see only the street, bare, dirty, narrrow, scorching and familiar.

It was our universe. We were so absolutely the street's children that, by the time we were three, the quarter held no secrets from us. And at ten, we knew about women, as the prostitutes – whom we could have for a few réals – lived openly amongst the respectable inhabitants of Azrou. Everyone knew about them. I remember:

When I was eleven, an older friend took me to a brothel for my initiation into the thousand and one secrets of the flesh. The women made us tea, which we paid for in advance, but did not give us time even to taste it. A half-naked woman beckoned me to follow. I was very tense: in imagination, already wrapped in her flesh, almost drowned between her expert legs like a puppet drifting on the waves. I felt an ache in my belly. I was going to touch that sombre shape and revel in it. Encouraged by Allal Rifi's winks, I followed.

Now Azrou would yield to my curiosity. The woman led me to a cell where the only light came from a tiny hole in the wall; it was more of a spy-hole than a window. She asked for money, holding out her right hand and ceaselessly massaging her fallen breasts with her left. I paid up.

The wall behind us was in shadow. On the hard beaten-earth floor were a plate and silver tea-pot, a cracked chamberpot, and a nasty towel. The mattresses were arranged in rows like beds in a boarding school dormitory. This was done for the great days of maximum activity, market days and days when the soldiers were on leave. 'When the beast in man is unleashed, shame can hang itself.'

The mattresses were arranged so that, during rush hour, the clients were simultaneously poised in rows on their prey. All shame and modesty vanished.

After a pause the men would chat together, comparing notes on their animal activities and the women's finer points. . . Friendships were occasionally struck up on the blood- and sperm-stained mattresses; dubious friendships always leaning towards vice. Moments of revolting orgy, collective sensuality, movements of ravaged flesh, rivers of sperm illicitly spilt between anonymous legs that were open all the time, always

72

open wide as windows in an empty house. It was said they would perform your wildest fantasies for a little extra money.

An icy hand was laid on my shoulder and I found myself sitting on the edge of the bed.

'All right, have you made up your mind? I don't have time to waste. . .'

It was not impossible that he had been in there himself.

'Listen, you stay here and I'll come back in a minute. I could be having one or two others while you're making up your mind. . .'

She left. I did not dare hold her back. Didn't I want simply to be alone, thinking of nothing, ridding myself of my anguish?

I stretched out on the ground. I was frightened of the room and its bed, hollowed out by so many bodies; frightened of that woman, heavy with dusty dreams and useless sperm; frightened of being devoured by her sex. I had been badly prepared for this catastrophe and did not have the necessary courage. These thoughts wore me out, and I shut my eyes.

Father was lying on the bed alongside the same woman, mocking my undersized penis. I was choking with impotent rage. The monster was laughing. The woman beside him was stroking his great chest, kissing his hairy hand, and singing snatches from a Berber song. I jumped up. The wreck had returned and put her clammy hand on my hand on my stomach.

'Well, little one, have you made up your mind?'

Father had vanished and the woman before me wasn't the one who had just been lying on the bed with him. I was relieved.

'Listen, boy! I'm being very patient with you because I like you and it's the first time I've had a kid your age. . .'

A kid! So I was nothing but a beginner!

'. . . but if you don't want to do it, if you're scared, you can go. Stop wasting my time!'

I looked at her for a long moment and could not find any expression at all in her eyes. It was a closed, flat face, one of those dark faces that do not say a word. Her eyes were large but extinct: hollow eyes, almost dead. I asked:

'Have you been to bed with my father?'

She burst out laughing and I could see her black teeth.

'Your father! Who *is* your father? I've been to bed with the whole world. It's my job and I know every prick in the town. . .'

She spoke these last words very simply. I could not look at her teeth again. I chased my frozen dream:

'My father is Ba Driss, the carpenter.'

My answer was not out before she started her thick laughter again. This time I could not avoid her black teeth.

'Si Driss – "Honey" Driss! Of course! A bastard, that "Honey". Of course I know your father. Wait – I even know your one-eyed uncle. There can't be a prick in the whole town that hasn't been up here.' (She accompanied the words with a gesture.)

There was still mine, at any rate. Would I be the only one not to know bliss with this woman? I looked straight into her eyes and was surprised to spy a little gleam flickering on her face, as fleet as lightning. Then her face again became as flat as her stomach.

'Tell me, is he really your father?'

She held my wrist and I knew she was being kind to me.

'You know I've no reason to lie to you, little one. Your father is a shit and I'll tell you this: he even promised to marry me. He said I made love better than any woman he knew. I refused to marry him when I discovered he had kids.'

She turned me over gently on to the bed. Which creaked. Sooner or later I would have laid down so that she could deafen me with her words. So Father had been here already. A deft hand brushed along my body and paused for a moment on my crotch. Lying close to this whore, I felt my heart beating fast. A painful tremor shook me. I was going to know woman at last! I would know the darkness and be able to talk about it as an insider. My passion was out of control.

'Come, little one, are you afraid of. . .'

74

I did not let her finish. I knew what she was going to say, and scrambled to my feet and yanked down my trousers. I wanted to prove *I* could have her just as my father had done. She would tell him, of course, and he must not be able to think it had been a failure. I could go as far into this woman as he had. I threw myself on the filthy body and kissed its hair, its neck, the pillow. . . The animal in me had to prove to this body and to my father that I could be ferocious too. I suddenly found myself trapped between two powerful legs. I was enveloped and struggled awkwardly to force a passage into her ravaged flesh. I was going to hurt this woman – destroy her! Stretched beneath me, legs spread, she let me do it. Then, seeing I could not manage alone, for all my good intentions, she slid a hand between our bodies and helped me. I was sweating, blowing, gasping. . . her hand was searching.

The childhood of every boy in Azrou ran aground on these hard, grubby beds, between the witches' fleshy thighs. Like the rest, I was going to sow my wild oats in the pit of oblivion, throw myself blindly into the darkness of my deliverance, roll over and over in this act of liberation. Now I would be a true man in my bestiality.

The body under me had stopped moving. I felt this, and it desolated me. I was perching on a sunken torso that showed no signs of life or warmth. Despite this anguish, I made a final attempt to trample the path that had been soiled by the man I hated, and I managed to touch her sex. It was shaved. A horrible sensation. I don't know why, but it reminded me of an arsehole.

The weary body reached out a transparent hand towards a gob of chewing-gum stuck to the wall, picked it off, put it in its mouth and began chewing. The other hand was still digging.

Father was a shit, like all fathers. The Kechla was a place for shits and whores. Now I had become a little shit myself: this act promoted me from innocence to the ranks of true shittiness.

The *chergui* was blowing outside. The walls and ceiling were sweating. This stone, staring at me, outlasting my act and my insubstantiality, was witness to my hallucinations. The flies were excited by the heat and stink, and buzzed around my hollow head, making me giddy, mating now and then on the pillow or the wall before they vanished.

The heat was overpowering. A smell of garlic suddenly filled the room and suffocated me. I hated garlic because Father ate it. At least a dozen raw cloves every morning. Someone had recommended it for high blood pressure. His breath would have felled a rhinoceros. How disgusting Father was. I was slyly avoiding him these days. I got up before him and left early for school; the cool morning air was good for doing my homework. In the evening I went home and straight to bed. I always had an excuse – toothache or a bad stomach. There were never any serious objections. My parents did not really care about my health.

Garlic! The smell was everywhere, sticking to my skin like leprosy. It was sickening. The body under me was still chewing its gum. Its hand was still groping. No life at all, not even a glimmer of life, and that smell clutching my throat. Garlic was cheap and Father stocked up as often as possible. His pockets were full of it and he kept it in all his drawers, throughout the house. What a stink! Poor Mi, having to share his bed. Mi was all submission. No rebellion. She had no rights, not even the right to breathe a little louder.

Father's success puzzled me and his good luck exasperated me. His many accidents had not sapped his will to live. He was solid and hard as rock. Indestructible, perhaps? I'd have given half my life to break down the substance of him. Father's death would have ended our worries, or mine at least – a harvest which fate stubbornly refused to yield. Growing up demanded ordeals and dense hatred. Life never granted us favours.

In all her Moroccan woman's desolation, Mi knew how to keep quiet. She also knew how to weep. She was like all women of her kind, for whom there were two great womanly virtues: knowing how to weep discreetly and how to preserve a noble silence. She was proud, yet her pride did not lie in her knowledge but in her patience, silence and resignation. Mi kept her suffering in – and to – herself.

All at once I felt very tired, loaded with sleep. Hazy images floated before my eyes, and a swarm of thoughts boomed in my head like distant thunder. I was about to doze off when someone grabbed me by the hair:

'Well, are you going to do it?'

Impatient and brutal. Swept along by my nightmare, I had utterly forgotten her. She was still there, flat out beneath me: a plank, a board of flesh and bone. I made a last effort and managed to shift my weight on to my elbows, eyes half-shut. I made a few clumsy movements to show the body I was definitely going through with it. It was Friday, a holy day, God's day. The children had all arranged assignations in debauched places like this. Always on Fridays, for the grown-ups honoured the Lord's day. They could disguise their innate hypocrisy so well. So the children were free to do as they liked; it was their holiday. As for me, I would come back some other day purposely to meet my father in the uproar of the brothels and challenge him there.

The family's agony was too heavy to bear. I had always waited for a miracle, for a radical change in our way of living. Life before and behind us was a tangle of brambles and thorns. We could not move without cutting ourselves. From day to day Mi gradually burned herself up like a waxen statue in sunlight. Now she was so thin as to be transparent. That was her fate.

Father was putting on weight; he was flourishing. The few curls left on his head were tended painstakingly by Mi, who was saddled with that particular task. The scissors were sharp and Father's neck was regularly bared to my fantasies. It was also her job to rid his body of lice. Father liked to fatten the tiny animals before letting them loose on us. Mi crushed them between her thumbnails and our fingers were stained with their blood. When the frying pan was on the stove, she sometimes held them between finger and thumb and called one of us to open our hand and take them alive before dropping them on to the hot metal.

Mi warned us not to clash with the patriarch. Yet we did not know how to free ourselves from our deep hatred of him. We were afraid of him – of him first, then of God – and did not want to risk changing anything. That would not have been any use. There was a void in our deepest being which he had put there. And we were dependent on his bad will and his unstable, bombastic character.

Everything was cold, even the marble body I held beneath me, which I was possessing and mastering with my own skinny body. I was completely empty. All the innocence of my youth would die at the end of this silence, beyond flesh and ejaculation. I was going to know the adults' madness, and knowing this gave me a sick pleasure that warmed my soul with pride.

My whole body shook to the tip of my being. I knew this animal communion was a passing consolation, but I hung on with all the strength of my withered childhood. I was still in control but knew I would not resist for long. I didn't want to move. Energy and effort had died in me before they had even been born. And exhaustion. . . an old man's death always used to make me happy: 'That's one less pig on the earth!' Inevitably I was thinking of my own death, and was afraid – afraid above all at that moment: imagine dying at the point of calamity!

While the lifeless body was busy with its malignity, my spirit suddenly sank. I stopped wanting to travel deeper into this mysterious, hostile desert and realized all at once I was not doing anything: I was just pretending. I stayed like that for two hours and understood bitterly that I was not yet confident and wise enough to voyage into the adults' night. I had the sudden, strange feeling that my youth and innocence were abandoning me. I pushed my hand into the void, and my fingers touched time's wrinkles. I did not know how to find refuge in the hole which was waiting to be rescued. I was already less proud of myself and wondered whether I could get away from the flesh and become myself again. God and his Prophet must have abandoned me, and I wanted to redeem myself by pissing as much as I could on this sperm- and curse-

78

swollen body; but it would not have been any use. And I wanted to scream, thump and hurt it. . . That wouldn't have been any use either. There was nothing left but to go forward. That was my way out and my deliverance.

'Love is no sin', they say, 'but you must love openly and joyfully. It is only sinful when you hide away and are unhappy.' And I was sinful and ashamed. I had had to choose and had chosen to find freedom through life's sewers. I was intrigued and contaminated at the same time. And the time had come to open my eyes in the night of my solitude, but I preferred to keep them closed because as long as I did so, I could always turn back. I was scared.

I started trembling. I was no more than an ache, and did not understand what was happening in me. I wanted to run away and preserve my pain as long as I could. I wanted to be a scalpel and cut this flesh and make it bleed, I wanted. . . By the time I realized what was happening, it was over. Limbs broken, I sank into oblivion – that was my strange deliverance. My penis shrank. I was just a puppet and already indifferent.

The flies still buzzed round me. What a mess! The flesh beneath me streamed with sweat and sperm. I saw that I had somehow achieved my first orgasm. An act of faith.

I had always hoped my father would vanish: an accident or illness. . . After my defeats I had very quickly understood my powerlessness. Also I could not think beyond the possibility of an accident or illness.

The woman's body slept beneath me, legs spread wide, like a dog in the sun. So much had happened and she had not noticed any of it. She was sleeping, and stupid with sleep, loaded with such tiredness, burdened with so many years' waiting and sinning.

Sometimes Mi looked like that when she was asleep with her legs apart, and that disturbed me, as she disturbed me when she wore her baggy red trousers. Mi was modest. She never mentioned her periods to Father. She simply put on her loose red trousers or her red scarf, and father understood; Mi was impure and had to sleep alone. She was spurned for the duration of her periods.

There was no talking in our family – only doing. Mi wore her red trousers and Father understood that it was stormy at sea. So he could go freely to the Kechla. Mi only resumed her place in the conjugal bed after visiting the *hammam*. She washed, perfumed herself with flower-water, applied khôl, brushed her teeth with *souak*, wore her new *mansouria*, and opened her legs that night for Father's penis and gave herself, as usual, in silence and darkness.

Mi was always modest, and modesty was part of the education she drummed into us. Father was modest too whenever he could be, whenever he wasn't angry. And as he was not often in a good mood, our education was extraordinarily barbarous.

I did not know whether to get up or stay lying down. I looked ridiculous in this position. The body slept on. As if it had no part in all this. Just my luck. The first time I managed to put a stop to my anguish, I had to exorcise myself in a body more dead than alive: in a rotten whore.

The town's whole heat was in me, and I sweated as never before. I was being martyred and felt I was in hell. Surely the pagan Arabs were right to believe the birth of a girl-child was a curse and bury her alive. Why had times changed? I could have been spared this ordeal, which was so savagely disproportionate to my weakness and sexual inexperience. I was ashamed of pouring out my first vitality in this pointless way, on a corpse.

I asked myself a thousand questions. Those very questions I never found answers for because I never had the right to explanations. Everything to do with sex was taboo. And even mentioning it was forbidden. Our education consisted of always saying 'yes', 'thank you', and kissing the grown-ups' hands. It was impossible to break that law, and I was deeply humiliated because I knew I was incomplete. We were trained to respect the elders and their traditions. We had the street to satisfy our curiosity, where we learned through violence all we needed for our young requirements. But something was missing. Lots of things. Things I should have had or known and neither had nor knew. Now I knew I had deceived myself in looking for salvation in this place.

At that age I did not know how children came into the world. I was sure their parents either bought or found them. Father often said he had found me in a rubbish-bin. That was his way of joking; his jokes were rubbish. (Was I the flood- or dustbin-child?) It didn't take me long to see how true it was: Mi was Father's rubbish-bin and had given him a scrap of waste which he decided to call Abdelhak. He found Hafid, then a sister, then another whom he called Mariame. That surprised everyone: it was a foreign name, not a common one in Azrou. I was not allowed to ask questions and that suited me very well. I knew it would have been no use anyway. When Father spoke or made a decision, however stupid, we had to listen and blindly obey. For Ismaïl the Noble, the Generous – had he not obeyed his father who wanted to cut his throat as a sacrifice to the heavens? We had had to follow his example ever since.

Our life consisted of obeying and respecting adults. So I had to obey God the Father, and tolerate the gossip about 'Laligou's daughter', as people called her, before they started referring to her as 'Marie' so as not to make any mistakes. I wondered what Father had in mind, naming her that; he never did anything without reason.

'It's a pretty name and I like it,' he said. Which did not convince me. He must have had a scheme and I soon discovered what it was: he wanted to win the good will of the French colonists and was succeeding very well. 'Laligou' offered us tins of jam, sweets, chocolate, biscuits, etc. Father had earned Christian friendship and charity – and the hatred of Azrou at the same time. People became hostile. Hafid and I had to put up with all sorts of mean tricks at school and in the street. Mi ignored it all. The women were more subtle than the men and sarcastically praised my sister's beauty. Some claimed she had the hair of a *Roumia* and others dwelt on her eyes. 'French eyes', they said – as if eyes could be 'made in France' or 'made in Morocco'. Mi took their compliments as sacred truth and thanked them. She was happy, and the sincerity of her happiness only increased my frustration. Father was proud of this latest victory over the people of Azrou: it was revenge. Naming her Marie had brought him closer to the nazarenes, so he did not have to endure any more hypocrisy or ingratitude from people. The only ones who spoke to him now were those who could not do without him. This general reaction made life even more difficult than it already was, especially for Hafid and me. Fortunately the hostility only lasted a few months, and time gradually restored things to their former state, as it always does. The incident over, people felt free to choose foreign names – even bizarre ones – for their babies.

The bed creaked like a rotten bone, and the air was almost unbreathable. Once more I was shaking with the anger and spite of the defeated. Vague ideas swarmed through my fevered head, and I felt something new: a desperate need to run away from this body, crumpled by male stupidity, and not even wait for it to come round. I knew I could not face its black teeth again. I glanced back as I was leaving and was horrified to see a thread of blood seeping between the woman's thighs.

The body was still stuck to the bed. I vowed never to return to the Kechla – even swore aloud that this would never happen again. I was still a child and could not know that this squalid place was essential for our development. I was soon back in the brothels, searching for myself between the legs of some prostitute oppressed by the shadows of barrenness. I so wanted to stop at my first sexual disappointment, but was lost deep in the maze of desire.

My body revolted me. I was like a hunted dog, and my

shame was mixed with rage. I felt guilty not because I had performed like a beginner, but because I wanted more. I sank deeper and deeper into the hell of flesh and had no strength left to continue my journey into the darkness of virginity. All the same I eventually reached the end of my dream and discovered, without much difficulty, animal instinct. I was already imagining the day – imagining it with sick delight – when I, like everyone else, would have access to Messaouda.

From the very beginning of history God's flail has brought the blind and pride-sick to his feet. Remember that, and kneel.

– Albert Camus

Messaouda is no more. Messaouda is dead. The news spread quickly. She died in the street one winter's night and was discovered the next day at dawn, frozen, half-naked in the white snow. She died as our dogs die, alone in the snow, cold, hungry and wretched. She was dead – certainly dead this time.

The adults were so shaken by the unexpected death that they did not know what to do. Messaouda dead: it was unthinkable! Life without her was hardly imaginable. She looked very ordinary on her deathbed; she might have been sleeping. People did not dare believe they had actually lost their dark companion. Their voices were tearful, and for once their talk about her was generous.

'She isn't dead,' said some. 'It's a cruel joke!' Her whole life had been nothing but a bad joke.

They gathered round to pay their last respects to the thing, the mutilated corpse that had given them so much fun. What would they do now with their blank days? Who would tell the women tales of blood and sperm? What sights could the street now offer the children? Messaouda was like the great wheel of time which turned life in Azrou. And what a life it was! Even Father wept. He would weep for anything that wasn't worth his tears. His brief weakness cheered me and I suddenly saw that my fear of him was simply prejudice. Perhaps he did *not* embody the definite image of God and was like everybody else: vulnerable. So I didn't have to be afraid of him. I took my image of him and tore it up.

A fat, helpless old man approached the corpse, which had been laid on an old blanket. He turned to the crowd and, stirred by a sense of his own uselessness, whispered 'Let us pray for her soul!' A dog barked. The people drew closer to the body in bleak silence. The old man led the prayer for the dead. Farther off, two men waited with their donkeys. It was an interminable prayer. Still farther off, the women were stiffly upright in the cold, wailing, tearing their hair, clawing their faces; as was traditional. We children watched the rhythmic despair gripping our mothers and throwing them into frenzy, and picked up things they were shedding in their trance. They had no dignity in the face of death. The procession got under way. The women were surprised by the men's approach and fled with an appalling din.

The corpse was put on the back of a donkey. The men following were strangely disciplined, chanting the burial litany. The women had miraculously vanished; they were never allowed to follow the dead to the cemetery on the burial day. In their hypocritical prayers the men begged the Almighty to spare Messaouda from hell fire. They dreaded hell, but we didn't know what it was. We were taught at the *m'sid* that it was a horrible thing.

A crow fell stone dead from the sky in front of the procession as it passed the spring at Titahcen. The frightened donkey stopped before this strange apparition and could not be beaten into movement. A bad omen. The men gathered in the snow, prayed again, and argued about the bird. A coincidence? – Out of the question. No, it was the hand of Fate. Some people said the wretched Messaouda was damned; the ominous bird meant that hell was certain: even the donkey sensed damnation. A logical explanation of the phenomenon must be found, to banish all suspicion and convince consciences both good and bad.

'It was dead and hanging from a branch – the wind blew it down just at that moment, that is all,' suggested the fat old man.

Ingenious, but it would not do. There were no trees nearby. Each new explanation was more absurd than the last. The men were floundering when, finally and reluctantly, they admitted the possibility of a heavenly premonition. It was a sign, a black sign. Some people were afraid of being damned themselves, and disappeared. I watched father closely: he was in the middle of the crowd and he alone interested me. He kept spitting into the neck of his *djellaba* to ward off evil, clicking his beads and praying aloud.

There was a final consultation, then they agreed what to do. Messaouda could not be left on the donkey for ever, nor deprived of the rites due to the dead. The will of heaven might turn against the entire town, and it must not be crossed any further. In prayer and fear, a wise decision was taken. The fat old man found a piece of white cloth and threw it over the bird. The others lined up behind him and joined in a prayer no less impassioned than before.

After much hesitation they drew lots to decide who should bury the bird. There was a frightful grin of relief on Father's face; he was safe. I was disappointed. The unlucky one came slowly forward. Tears streamed from the holes in his head. He turned to the others and looked at them frantically. Nobody came to help him. The man realized he would get no support. He advanced by little tottering steps, swayed, reached trembling arms towards the bird, yelled hoarsely, and fell dead a hand's breadth from the crow.

Then the men knelt down, prostrated themselves before the bird and kissed the frozen ground, rolling in the snow and quite forgetting to pray. The dead man was moved aside. Evil fate had not spared him! This test had been too much for a weak heart. Someone ran to find a black billy-goat. They slaughtered it in front of the bird. Hot red blood soaked into the snow.

The *moqqaddem* had heard the shouting. He arrived and went straight to Father, who quickly explained. The *moqqaddem* knelt in the snow, gabbled a prayer, stood up again, climbed on to a rock, and addressed the crowd.

'*Bslemah!* The compassionate one, the Merciful, the truth is come – falsehood is dead! Falsehood must die. Misfortune is with you: you brought it here, and you earned it. This fine sight is no mere accident. Our Lord God sent you proof of his curse today. You have lost your way and must pay the mortal price for your falsehood. . .'

Someone in the crowd collapsed like a sick horse. In the distance the women began screaming and smashing the silence. The *moqqaddem* surveyed his audience, and continued more bitterly:

'You must *act* if you don't want the heavens unleashed against you! Do what your ancestors instructed you to do at such times! Start by praying – on your knees!'

Again the men prostrated themselves in the snow beside the bird. The *moqqaddem* prayed. The air was heavy. The *moqqaddem* climbed back on to the boulder and continued his speech:

'Everything on earth passes away. Only God's face remains in its majesty and spendour. Who does good, though only an atom, shall know that face. Whoever commits evil, though only an atom, he also shall know it. . .'

An *Allah Akbar* spread through the crowd like wildfire, rising as if from a single throat, and rose to swell the clouds. The *moqqaddem* continued:

'Brothers!. . . No, you are no longer my brothers! The curse lies on you, it's on your wives and children, and on your withered balls. You live in sin and God's punishment will soon scourge your stupid heads like a hurricane. . .'

Eyes downcast. The crowd was buzzing; they were really frightened. The sky filled with black clouds. The air was too thick to breathe. The orator took the opportunity to spit out all his heart's hatred, and his voice was rich with contempt as he pronounced his threats:

'You have strayed from the path. God is not blind to your actions, nor deaf to your words. He sees you, he hears you, he watches you. He is Allah – fear his wrath!'

Pause.

'God is not respected in this part of his kingdom. He won't spare you his curse. You are damned. . .'

Our wretchedness was now official, ratified by the *moqqaddem*. He took off his *burnous* and threw it to his assistant. Battle was scarcely joined and it was going to be long.

'You are animals!'

There was no reaction to his taunts. The men were ready to pay for their sins. Sins there certainly were, and they must have been unforgivable for the adults to take these insults without a murmur.

'Allah abandons you to damnation! You are alone with the mortal sins you drag along the rusty rails of your miserable lives. In evil-doing you are unsurpassed. You have degraded this town, ruined it with your animal behaviour and your lust. . .'

A few more collapsed in the snow. Silence ruled, and it was unsettling. Now stifled sobs could be heard. Nerves were drawn tight. I wanted another drawing of lots. Father was bewildered. His cowardice exasperated me. If only he'd go away, disappear! But this time I took pity on him. They were slipping into hysteria. The *moqqaddem* went on:

'Look at yourselves, look at your women and children, look at your homes! . . .'

The company shivered. From fear, not cold. The *moqqaddem* raked the congregation with a vicious glare and continued his harangue:

'Look at your life! It's stale. And where is your morality? You squandered it between the legs of prostitutes. You don't love life any more. You have taken root in arrogance, promiscuity and vanity. . . Look at your hands, look at your pricks! They are filthy and disgusting. You have always enjoyed yourselves and neglected your Lord and Master's words: "Whoever does good, does so to his own advantage, and whoever does evil, does so to his own harm, and God is no tyrant over men". . .'

This *surah* was received with gloomy silence. The crowd was dumbstruck. The *moqqaddem* coughed. His words were devastating, and he knew it. Which was why he was determined to make this moment last. Not even a whisper of protest. I was a little envious, and lingered to find out where he would lead them next. He had plainly managed to plunge everyone in guilt and repentance. His voice rang out:

'You are only reaping what you sowed: which is sin. You are wrapped in sin up to the ears. How bitter your lives will be! Sin – you hoard it in your rooftops, in your hearts and eyes, in what you do and what you say. Your orgies in the Kechla have wrecked you. You are drowning in promiscuity and you have lost your way. You are flies swarming on a heap of turds! You are dogs! . . .'

His voice was shrill. The worst was yet to come. Now I was succumbing to the general disease as well.

'You wallow in the sewage of morality. And you are all together in this tragedy: I know you have bad consciences, but it's too late to correct this moral and religious chaos you have yourselves created. Too late, I tell you. Too late. . .'

The *moqqaddem* stopped to draw breath. He wiped his face and gazed at the crowd. Only the frank, surprised eyes of the children looked back.

'I make no prophecies. I don't condemn or judge you. My task is to warn you against the hell waiting for you now. The signs are clear. Don't wait for fate's favour or reprieve. Pray and prepare for the flood! Yes, the hour has come when each will be rewarded as he deserves. Taste the Fire – the cost of what you've done! . . .'

These last words were greeted with an angry *Sadaq Allah or Ladim*. Some people ran away to bolt the doors when they reached home. The rest stayed a long time, racked with despair and waiting for the *moqqaddem* to make a decision.

The men would meet at our house for supper after the last prayer. The *tolba* would recite verses from the Koran till dawn, sixty *hizb* at a time: 'He takes out the Selka.' They would have a collection and make a *qoubba* to bury the bird in. People would bring offerings and candles. It would help them solve their problems of money, health, or love. They would organize a *moussem* every year on the same day, and beg him to keep us safe from misfortune.

The *moqqaddem* was in a corner, silently counting the collection money on to his belly. The *tolba* were chanting the sacred word in nasal voices. Father, proud of being the chosen host, distributed mint tea to the company. The children, sitting cross-legged, filled the courtyard.

Some of the *tolba* were already asleep, lulled by the verses. The old ones listened, opening their mouths from time to time to utter the name of God or join in the end of a verse. They were carried away by the Koran's melody, sweetly rocking their wandering memories. Some were weeping, pierced by a longing for God.

Their throats full and faces dripping, the *tolba* doffed their caps now and then to wipe their heads, revealing skulls scored by time and ill-fortune.

The blind man sat in a corner, thinking about his wife. She had a lover. He was wondering how to get rid of him without arousing suspicion: the perfect crime. The poor wretch was found in the river a few days later, his sex cut off and his head smashed in. The authorities decided it was an accident.

The little fat man was planning his escape. He was going to leave his home and land and chase his old dream of bright lights and avenues flowing with cars.

Vile Jilali was thinking how to get his hands on his dead brother's belongings before disowning his nephews. With the *qadi*'s help, he could get the orphans' money for himself. The children would leave Azrou for the south, where they would run to seed with an aged aunt.

And Sidi L'yazid was dreaming of something very different. He was the worst shit ever to learn the Koran by heart. His wide-eyed stares loitered on the children's bodies, bruising their young flesh. The others laid plans to catch him red-handed and threw him out of the town.

Before he left Azrou the little fat man said to his wife:

90

'I haven't been well these last days. I'm going to Moulay Akkoub to bathe my old bones. Put out some food and clothing for me. Business is bad too. Times are hard. People don't die like they used to, more's the pity. When they're happy, people hardly ever call for us – they prefer the bands and *chikhats*. They want music and belly dancing. What times we live in! I'm going to put a candle on Moulay Driss's tomb and ask him to guide men back to the ways of the Lord. And I'll ask him for children, wife, to fulfil your life. How much longer will our night last? People don't even notice it. They are leaving the Prophet's path, they are lost. The mosques are empty – what times we live in! The end is near, "the signs are here". . . I'm going, wife. I'll be praying for the *Ch'rif* to protect us. I won't be gone long, goodbye wife! . . .'

He never came back.

What most struck me about those people was the ease with which they mapped out our history: the same history in which we were later to lose our way. Sometimes they lit our path, but often we had to struggle alone in a closed world of stifling truths. They sacrificed us in the name of a mystery education.

Every day and before our eyes, our parents did the very things forbidden to us and expressed attitudes we were not permitted. These contradictions drew us into a life of hopeless suspicion. We had no experience and we needed certainties.

The children kept their eyes open despite their exhaustion and the time of night. We had to rise to the occasion and apart from anything else, avoid Father's wrath. The women were busy making couscous on the terrace.

Midnight! The *tolba* broke into the *Fatiha* while my one-eyed uncle passed the hand-bowl round the company. There was not enough water for everyone. The plates of couscous arrived.

'But where are the tables?' shouted Father.

A moment's pause. A *taleb* got up to help me bring a big, round table into the middle of the room. The *tolba* set to work almost immediately, fighting over the meat before thrusting their fingers into the hot dishes. Out on the terrace One-Eye teased the fat toothless cooks, and pinched their great buttocks when his wife's back was turned.

All you could hear in the room were the unpleasant noises of chewing and snuffling. The supper was gone in a second and I was called to clear the table. The *tolba* licked their fingers, complimented my father, and wiped their hands on their *djellabas* before continuing their reading. There was some discreet snoring. Then time passed too quickly.

The muezzin called for the first prayer. Everyone got up, men and children stumbling sleepily. The dazed adults lined themselves up anyhow, and took their places in the first rows. The youngest were at the back; the children were paying for the adults.

The *moqqaddem* led the prayer and it seemed interminable. Our fatigue showed in the fluffed lines and our disjointed movements. Hafid fell asleep in the middle of the prayer. Sagging bodies flickered, like drunken ghosts. It was a shambles. I was streaming with sweat. Suddenly I felt sure that the closed world in which the adults kept us locked was about to explode in a storm of violence that would sweep away old age.

Everyone collapsed after the *Tahya* and went to sleep on the bare ground. The men were tucked up in their *djellabas* like old bundles. The children were shaking with fear and cold and slept on top of each other, in a pile in the corner. A few blankets were thrown over the older bodies. The women slept in another room. Only One-Eye was awake.

A little later I heard voices in the courtyard. Uneasy and curious, I crept to the door and stopped, shocked. At first I thought it must be a bad dream – hoped desperately it was only that. But I wasn't asleep. I knew One-Eye was capable of any imaginable wickedness but had not ever thought he would sink so low.

No, I wasn't asleep! He was crouching in a corner of the

yard with his trousers down and little Saïd before him – Saïd the widow H'lima's son, just twelve years old. He had hitched up his little ragged *djellaba* and was holding it between his teeth.

How true it is that no two acts of violence are ever the same. One-Eye was tightly gripping little Saïd and pushing his penis into him. Saïd was struggling. I wanted to vomit before hurling myself at the depraved One-Eye and strangling him. My world crumbled around me. My heart sealed against respect for the family, against the whole cult of the family and against all the other elements of my world. The reasons for my unconditional surrender to the adults disintegrated there and then at the sight of that rape. Adults were no longer my demi-gods.

The memory of Hafid and Abdou rose up and overturned the scene before me, and I felt a fever in my stomach. The night's virtuous indifference seemed shameful.

Crime does not pay, especially when children are the victims. Little Saïd shrieked in the half-light. Then stifled sobs. How I pitied One-Eye in his grotesque position. I did not see the cat leap from the court-yard window, but the tiny noise made One-Eye start. We looked at each other and hatred flashed between us, cold and brutal as his bestiality. He looked away. In his shame he got to his feet and pulled his *djellaba* down over his balls. The madman had the nerve to look up again and pin me with a long stare, perhaps to intimidate me, and he started towards me as he did whenever he caught me out or felt like letting himself loose on my body. At any other time I would probably have fled. But it was different now. I had the strength to face him.

Little Saïd was in his corner, still clenching the hem of his *djellaba* tightly between his teeth. He had not yet realized just what had happened. His thin legs were trembling in the darkness. One-Eye was near me now: I felt his breath on my face, roaring in my ears, filling my head. I looked straight into his eye. I was not afraid of his stare or his rage. I forced him to lower his eye and the hand raised to slap me. I didn't move. His whole body was shaking. I felt him shrinking and dwindling before my glowing hatred. Had I wanted, I could have crushed him like a flea. He mumbled a few unintelligible words, kissed my forehead, groped in his pockets and thrust a few coins at me.

'Buy yourself some sweets and dates,' he gasped. 'Next market day I'll get you a ball and drum. You haven't seen anything, you were dreaming, that's all! I don't want any scandal, understand? Your aunt would not take it well. Go and lie down. . .'

I gazed at him for some time, then spat on the ground. In the darkness his face paled. The bastard was afraid of scandal and afraid of his wife and was buying my silence with chickpeas and raisins. He was afraid of me. I had him!

Saïd finally let go of his *djellaba* but still did not move. One-Eye was still holding out his money. I turned and went to my place, looking for my lost sleep and not finding it. Little Saïd came and lay down beside me and I felt his frozen, trembling limbs against my body. I turned over and hugged the corrupted innocent to my chest. One-Eye said a prayer aloud in the courtyard before he joined the sleepers.

It was almost dawn and I could think clearly: One-Eye could have hit me, woken the others and told them he had discovered me with Saïd. Nothing was beyond him. What was my word worth against his? The shock must have muddled him and I thanked God for sparing me the adults' injustice.

Father was first up and he woke everybody else. They remembered they had forgotten the final prayer last night, and lined up behind the *imam* to start the prayer again.

From that point One-Eye never left me alone. He was always at my elbow, buying me chickpeas, raisins, Barbary figs, marbles. . . he stuffed me with titbits and gave me a few sous now and then to pay my way in the Kechla. Occasionally he even came too and presented me to his friends, declaring that he wanted to guarantee my education as a man. That made me laugh.

The women awoke and made tea for us before we went out

into the snow to take the Bird and Messaouda to their last resting places. We left the house in silence. Saïd was in front of me and he scratched his buttocks through his woollen *djellaba*.

One-Eye held my hand. The last spadeful of mud was thrown on to Messaouda's coffin, and each went his own way home.

After that upheaval there was no truth left in the town. None, ever again.

In spite of his baseness I want you
to take pity on this enemy of his own
kind, this heart devoured by hatred
and avarice.

—François Mauriac

Some time after Messaouda's death, Father pawned his stone
mask and revealed his nocturnal face. I thought, 'It's a passing
fit, just lust for a woman.' But no, it was serious. At a stroke
he sold all he had and left his land and family to chase his
dreams and madness, and settled some thirty kilometres from
Azrou in the little village of El Hajeb, which was famous for
its prostitutes.

Father left us without any awkwardness or regret and went
in search of new hairless groins. Mi fought the move strenu-
ously, with all the strength of her tears. But she eventually
accepted her status of abandoned female, faced as she was with
the might of ruthless people who served neither law nor justice,
but the powerful ones, the rich and the 'right' people of Azrou.
We were neither rich nor 'right'. Father had money; the law
was on his side.

Mi was treated like a bitch and an ass when she went to
claim her rights and was soon shown the door by a notorious
qadi. She dried her tears at the brink of her new life.

Without warning or transition we were homeless, penniless,
and fatherless. From now on we were street-children, thrown
to every ill wind. Fate blew fiercely and carried us far, far from
Azrou, very far from Messaouda's tomb. Mi was flattened by
the blast and surrendered again, accepting her woman's destiny
and letting a whole violent world of misery, cruelty, injustice

96

and silence crash down on our young heads, beneath the gaze of the Almighty.

Another town, another house, other faces, new memories and agonies. Our bodies drifted like dead leaves into oblivion and were blown towards perdition in the whirlwind of a nightmare life. My few friends all gave me the same advice:

'You must forget it or it will kill you. . .'

'That is all I ask. . .'

'Pack up your troubles. . .'

'Yes, you are right! Yet. . .'

'Here – have a cigarette, it'll do you good. . .'

'And the others? It's very well for me but I can't forget everyone else. Do you think there's a way out?'

'We're meeting at Bouchahda's tonight. Come along – that will put things in a different light!'

The bedroom smelt of *kif*. Butts filled the shoe-polish-tin ashtrays. Scattered shoes and a few revolting socks. The light from a hundred-watt bulb filtered into the dim depths of a bottle of coarse red wine, which became our light and oblivion. A reptilian cat stared at us. Bouchahda kicked it. Well aimed. The cat did not move, nor even miaow: its back was broken. A few dirty glasses beside the *sebsi* and the pile of *kif*. Soon the *kif* would be smoked, the wine drunk, and everything transformed into passion or escape.

The happy crowds choked the street. Someone opened a window for air, and voices alternately clear and confused reached us from outside.

'More peaceful and there was more food too, back in the fourteenth century. . .'

'These damned hippies are to blame, I tell you. . .'

'The *fqih* predicted it. There's no respect any more, no shame either. What an age this is! . . .'

'*Ih Alyam*! Where is all the happiness and prosperity they promised us? . . .'

'When you can't tell the difference between a man and a

woman any more. . .'

'Bread already costs thirty-five francs, meat one and a half thousand, five francs won't buy anything any more. We are God's children and we'll return to him. . .'

'I tell you it's because of these cursed hippies. We've lost our faith. . .'

'And the men at the top are to blame but it's the beast that bears the burden. . .'

'There's no shame any more! Women show their faces, girls show off their thighs, boys wriggle their arses and have long hair. . .'

'It's the age of chewing gum, what do you expect? . . .'

'The world is upside down, *Yah latif*! Put eggs in water and the bad ones rise to the top. It is the same with us. God damn the unjust. . .'

'Curse the devil and keep your head down. . .'

'There's nothing but dirt 'twixt finger and nail. . .'

Impossible dreams filled the glasses and the *chqaf* of the *sebsi*. Giant birds flapped out of the forest and vanished in a chant of images. Nightingales skimmed the jasmin-covered ground and flew off to lose themselves in my farthest memories. Rivers of milk and honey parted at my curiosity. The gardens were strewn with golden fruit. Houris held out their arms to me while I played in a dream of pink and blue. The moon lapped my feet. The waves of a shoreless sea lay down before my wanderings. Laughter billowed along my naked body, filling my pores and my wounds. Lovely birdsong caressed the day. Airborne breasts and lips fluttered like feathery butterflies in a paradise of flowers and enveloped the world in joy. Light-footed gazelles danced and vanished in a shower of light.

When the curtain fell on my dreams I rediscovered my anguish, shaking at the edge of my stunned consciousness. I comforted it as best I could and it took up its old place in my memory, settled itself and began fouling the depths of a dream which was meant to counteract it. It always ended the same

98

way after fighting the invisible demons of my imagination: I surrendered my lucidity and fell back into the pit of oblivion. I seemed in spite of everything to be away from myself very much of the time, and it was unbearable – no doubt because of the fatal, echo-filled calm which bruised my raw consciousness every time. I was not allowed to escape, even escape myself, alone.

I sank disgustedly into the street-sweepings of life, well aware of the dangers around me when I met God at the dead of night, saving me from certain destruction. Sad to say, that had not stopped me dragging silent apathy on board the battered raft of my fallen life.

Mi, only half conscious, half senseless from the blows of fate, did not quite realize what was happening. I believe she even expected this deadly storm; had always expected and prepared for it. But not I.

My hopes and plans would not come to anything now. I did not have the right to give up; that would have been cowardice. I was chosen to take command after the shipwreck. Mi had given birth to a 'man' who had to prevent our image from changing. He pawned his plans, put on a stone mask far too big for him, and made his words and smiles lie with the tenacity of a monkey and the nonchalance of a stray dog. His mother was too proud of him to understand that destiny was tearing out the best of him. He was no longer free in his joy or pain. Now he belonged to speech: he did not belong to himself at all any longer. So I left God behind, when I turned the corner into a new life fraught with ambushes and responsibility, and continued alone. My will ached for space, freedom, the wind, open roads. . . and died of despair and useless effort.

I became the sixth pillar of Mi's faith, without which the other five could never bear up. Mi had faith in the same way she had tears and troubles. She usually prayed five times a day. Mi – fasting, frozen and transparent, wrapping herself in nobility and devotion, submitting to long days of hardship, *zakate*, pilgrimage.

Mi belonged to society's dark side. Hers was the tribe of the uprooted whose stillness set time out of joint. And the dark side of society is the side of shame, silent tears, unspoken words. The illegitimate side looking into cursed silence and finding the weakness, isolation and anonymity where it flounders and drowns. Mi was exempt from the *zakate* because she had nothing to give. So she did not receive anything. She still had her pride and there was no question of our taking alms: Mi had dignity in our wretchedness. The evil wind had sheared our cable and set us adrift, but her hand and eye were still steady. As for the pilgrimage, some lost souls claimed it was nothing but a madhouse, a carnival where religion was an excuse for doing business. In her helplessness Mi believed them.

Fate's mocking treachery put us in an illegal position. It had happened! Fate was dividing us for ever at this turning point of our lives, and the gates of chaos slammed on the hypocrisy of our 'happy family'.

It was on a Friday.

A holy day.

The Lord's day.

My life as a man had dawned
with a black sun
and I was already weary

Mi, three times repudiated. This time it was final. The holy
book had already decided that: for ever. Mi had no illusions
left. Nor had we. Religion was absolute on this point: Mi had
been repudiated for the last time. It was written in black and
white on the divorce contract drafted by two official crooks.
The irreversible had happened. The Ogre had gone and the
Book been shut on his departure. Mi had taken down her
prayer beads and frayed our nerves every day with its incessant
rattle. And we left never to return. Night swallowed us, and
our night was eternal. The words were naked and plain: For
ever!

Mi had packed her memories in her baggage and dragged us
behind her. We went away encased in her solitude.

She prayed before we left at the tomb of the Bird that died
at Messaouda's funeral. She humbly knelt, kissed the muddy
ground, and lit some candles. Father had unsheathed his arrogant prick and gone to seek his frenzy in empty cunts. He
soon found wombs for his progeny.

I could guess what Mi said on the Bird's tomb.

'I am only a poor woman. You know I have done nothing
to deserve such a fate. My children are still little and the *qadi*
won't give us the food allowance that our religion grants. Driss
paid the *talaq* to be on his side. I know you are not like the
qadi, that's why I am here weeping on your tomb. I know
you alone can avenge me on the tyranny of fate. I beg you,
this Friday, the Muslims' day, to bring a great disaster on both

men. Typhoid for one and plague for the other. Give me a sign and I promise not to forget you on the *moussem*. I'll come back with an embroidered blanket for your tomb. I am tying a knot in my scarf, and the day it undoes itself I will know you have led me out of affliction by avenging me on the two men. You know I always kept my promises to you. Help me, avenge me and my children on Sid L'Ouali. . .'

In her woman's absurdity Mi lowered her head and regained the line of time. The sun shone down, blind with injustice and corruption, on innocent children. The line was inscribed on our mutilated bodies by the silence and abuse that piled up every dark day and doom-laden night of our lives.

The streets of Azrou swallowed up my sick memories in their dust, and veiled pride walked towards other horizons. The unknown waited patiently in the rock, in the earth, in the waves and the wind. . . Exile was irrevocable. The Book had decreed: it must be so. Hope had clamped down again on my illusions. Mi wept and suffered and pined, and we suffered with her in our agony and neglect.

Mi the repudiated wife, the rejected woman.

Tell me, tell us about the insult in your body, the open wound of your soul tatooed by social injustice – men's injustice. Tell us about shackled language and trembling speech. Tell me about your muzzled sex and the stains on your body, time's wound opening in you and engulfing us, the scar of shame and your wrinkles appearing before daybreak. Tell us about the night shutting in our horizons, the sea burned by the sun. Tell us about the newborn's violence in the silent night when the wife becomes a mother and suffering, when the baby turns to stone and everything else to ashes and smoke.

Tell me about the beach empty after the storm, and the uprooting after the wound, and the blood after the tearing, and the shame after the pain, and the scar. . .

Tell us about the split day, the dried-up well, the crippled fate, the child orphaned or abandoned, the fear and misery of our souls.

Tell me what lies beyond your speech, our thoughts, our

dreams of mountains collapsing on to your face, crushed by the first ordeal. Tell us about the lies and the sacred Book, the prayer-beads strung to our dreams, witness of time and our fate. Tell me about the grey splintered stone, the movement and distance of the sand-sculpted wave, the hour of your absence, your life slaughtered by storms of shame and disgrace.

Tell me about the knife in our flesh, tell me about injustice, the woman behind the wall, tell me about my mother.

Tell us about the word linking the gesture, the speech surviving the sacrifice. Tell us about the flaking walls, the extent of solitude, the sleep denied. Tell me about the timid cry, the miserly look beyond the ruins of time.

Tell us about the blood of the beast, the child and the virgin. Tell us about the innocent's tears, the deep wound, the infernal torture, the depth of our abyss.

Tell me, tell us. . .
Tell me, Mother, tell us!
Tell them about your silence, your blank eyes
Tell them about your resignation and your walled-up life
Tell them about your patience, prayers and abnegation
Tell them, tell them about Tomorrow
and about confusion.

In the transparent shadow-light of my youth, the parallel-breasted ghost shook with anger and impotence. Mi the animal-dream was trapped in her hatred and overwhelmed by our bottomless nightmare, or now and then by moody unpredictable distraction. Our thoughts crawled like snakes. No human feeling, no breathable life. The smile froze to a grin.

I remember one day when the family had gathered for tea, Father and my uncle had a bet: which of them would kiss his own wife's hand? My uncle hesitated for a long time, then dropped his wife's hand. She blushed with shame. But the Pig did his kissing enthusiastically, without a second's thought. This was when he was already drawing away from us. The birth-cord binding us to Father had already been damaged by life but it seemed to me that, just then and at one blow, fate cut the cord. I did not want to believe it. I knew we had made lots of mistakes in the past, and silence would never put things right. We had to talk, shout, scream and fight to the end, to keep our unity and identity. Our silence was always a weakness that Father exploited.

Everything had changed: looks and laughter, words and thoughts. We were no longer united against the worst but divided by the irony of fate and Father's madness. The conjugal yoke that Mi had kept in constant repair over the years lay in the ruins of our outworn memories. It was as if a sadistic destiny was determined to question again the image of this perfect, ambitionless couple: father was afraid and mother was submissive, while the children acquired their own share of shame and guilt. Mi knew the repudiation was final. She was equally sure the disastrous storm was about to burst on our heads.

Mi's prophetic fatalism was exasperating. All our discussions were based in uncertainty. The presence of fate in our daily life had left me with a sense of futility. 'This has happened because God ordained it. It must be thus and not otherwise!' Mi emphasized at each misfortune in our daily routine. This fatalism made me ill and clouded my youthful consciousness.

Despite the fact that our points of view were uncertain and unshareable, when I climb back up the slope of my past, I can find nothing in the deepest part of me but great warmth and admiration for that woman who is my mother. Along with this happy emotion my feelings for my father were indifference and silent hatred. For me as certainly for the others, he was only a wandering ghost in the wreckage of a distant past, paved with smothered passions and unshed tears.

We were rejected and mocked wherever we turned. It was as if we barely had the right to breathe while we waited to leave. When the Lord's voice thundered, heaven's gates closed. To stifle us and discourage us from talking and squabbling, the patriarch had almost-daily black rages and hurt us with the ease of a *tayaba*. His intractable arrogance had quickly throttled Mi's youth, marring her face with wrinkles and dulling her eyes, heavily ringed by the constant worries and responsibility of her situation. It must have been a premonition of the terrible fate awaiting her: a sign of petrifaction. We had to walk alone in the *chergui* which scorched our hopes. Father had cast off his sexual moorings. His hunt for young girls, impulse and frenzy, had begun.

Before we finally quit Azrou I went occasionallly to see Si H'mad the baker. I helped him 'turn the *tarha*' and in exchange he told me Father's story and the story of our county:

'A superiority complex, I tell you, born of an inferiority complex. Si Driss is a real bastard. I knew him better than anyone. . . an arse-licker and a runt. He never listened to anyone but the children of Sidna Issa. They gave him bad habits. They were his undoing – and yours.'

Si H'mad did know Father well: they lived together for years in Monsieur Capel's cellar. The three had had a verbal contract that the two friends held more dear than the Koran. Monsieur Capel warned them at the start:

'When you are here you are in my home. I can throw you out any time I please. Be in by eight o'clock and don't make any noise. And no alcohol or women. You will look after the house whenever I'm away. You must clean the stairs and do the gardening. Take it in turns to walk the dog. It goes without saying that you must always be available when Madame needs you to run errands. And empty the dustbin every morning. Those are my terms: you have to accept them and if I see any suspicious behaviour I'll destroy you. . .' The two men had accepted.

Mi had to bury her cross somewhere else. Azrou was as contemptible as ever and left us no illusions of a possible return. The future seemed diseased to us and we surely could and would not have any part in it. The heavens were still indifferent to our transition. Our fear? – Not knowing what tomorrow would bring.

We were relying heavily on some accident to destroy Father's resilient flesh; the electric lathe or saw might run amok, the gas-cylinder explode, the slate roof collapse, the drill leap up in his face. . . Whichever it was, only heaven would be responsible. We could not attempt anything ourselves because we lived in terror of public shame and disgrace: we were too cowardly to risk our petty tranquillity and specious calm. Mi demanded wisdom and prudence of us. We were her children, hence condemned to live in the shadow of her despair.

So we left our past. Mechanical heads creaked round us in the transparent darkness. Father enjoyed the results of his plotting. Mi's instinctive submission made him savagely egotistic; he had become a monster of egotism. There was nothing to do but drowse in our fever. Our muted rebellion made Mi nervous: we had to behave with dignity and accept calmly and resignedly – so she said – the wrong whose victims we were, and respond impassively to the leers and accusing looks, keeping our counsel and bowing our heads – as if we were guilty! How could our disgust and anger stay mute? Yet that was Mi's will. Submission. We had to submit to heaven's disdain and life's indifference, to the melancholy future and men's injustice, with dignity. We did submit.

From time to time I used to look at the photo album I had made from old shirts and cardboard that I found in the nazarenes' 'dustbin', where we went mostly on Sundays very early in the morning, and found all the delights which were missing from our lives. We brought back broken toys, cigarette butts, crusts, ragged but still wearable clothes, empty bottles, half-rotten vegetables and fruit. . . There too we first found our heroes Blec le Roc and Miki the Ranger.

In this vast area reserved for Christian rubbish, we masturbated together and even, at the height of our frenzy, raped one of the group – the weakest or youngest. If we were all equally matched we simply did the *nouiba* (one by one).

The nazarenes' dustbin was a goldmine, especially on Sunday. While 'they' were in church, praying upright and in their shoes, we revelled in the things we found and dug deeper into their filth.

As a little boy I used to dream of running barefoot through the dusty streets, rolling in the snow while the others warmed themselves at the stove, letting the sun burn my skin when the earth stopped spinning, yelling all my heart's obscenities at dead of night. . . But no. We had to submit with dignity, in the silence of our humiliation.

'Come here, my children!' said Mi once day. 'God is with us. Fear neither humility nor men, but only God who is Lord of all. Patience, patience, my children, and Allah will revenge us on their hardened hearts and closed minds, on men's stupidity. Don't lose yourselves in hatred. Don't do anything that religion forbids. Don't give in too quickly to your impulsive hearts. Think, my children, think before you act: truth and falsehood are never the same.

'Come here, my children, and say "I seek refuge with the Lord of the Dawn, away from the wickedness of living things and the dark night that overtakes us."

'Say:
"I seek refuge with the Lord of men
King of men
God of men
Away from spirits and men." Amen!'

Since our downfall Mi spoke little but always well. She had never talked before with such wisdom and serenity, though she was oppressed more than us by the pompous silence of male justice. Yet she had also slipped into a falsely prophetic attitude while the Old Man, regressing to second childhood, went freely about his nocturnal affairs.

I often enjoyed turning over those moments of my past that coincidence or chance had attached to my few photos. They were dirty and badly stuck down. I especially liked one of me holding hands with Monsieur Capel's daughter. Nicole was young, fresh, beautiful and always clean. I always cursed myself at the thought I was polluting the photograph with my presence.

When the French realized they had Father's loyalty, they helped him to get a patch of land and build a hut on it. It was there, as neighbours of the nazarenes, that we had to spend our time with Father.

I remember, one day. . .

Mi had to go away. She had quarrelled violently with Father and was going back to her family for a few days, hoping for their support. I was charged with keeping watch on the unchained Beast, as Mi was apprehensive and feared the worst. I was rather proud to dig in at home and upset Father's secret schemes. I had to deflect his tricks and hopes. I was there and Mi thought nothing could happen – thought she could 'sleep easy in her bed'.

Father came in with a dozen other people as I was making supper one evening. They went through the house and began to reckon up the value of the walls, doors and windows, the chairs, tiles, roof, lamps and nails. Everything was for sale. Ba Driss made loud jokes about our cold beds. In a second I felt the terror of the void into which he was going to tip us. His decision forced me to look at the threat hanging over us. I could only watch powerlessly as the human greed and meanness spread before my eyes.

Si H'mad had his own explanation of our wretchedness. He was convinced that colonization was responsible:

'The French are to blame, I tell you! They gave him their bad ways. I knew him when he was a brat from the *Mellah* and I've never known anyone as weak and low as he was. He'd give his arse for a smile from Madame Capel. Always servile, always useful, always sharp, always there. . . He's done me many a wrong. And I always said to him, "Who do they think they are? They are human beings like us. They are lucky enough to have been to school, but what is there to choose between, say, you and Capel?" And I said this too: "They are foreigners here. This great villa with its beautiful garden, that furniture, that car, this hole we rent – Capel did not bring them to Morocco in his suitcase. *We* gave him everything: money, luxury, a superiority complex, and the chance to exploit us. . ."'

I wondered, 'Where will we go when he sells the house?' I could not think of any one place that could hold all our un happiness. Then, in a transport of childish anger I fought the destructive fate that was crushing our fragile lives. I hurled myself against the world of hostility.

'This is not my son,' my father kept telling his companions. 'That bastard isn't mine. I disown him for ever, here before you. You are witnesses before God. Damn him and his mother and brothers till Judgement Day! He's a bastard, that vermin, he's a whore's boy. I curse him as the Prophet cursed his enemies. He's *my* enemy. I disown him here and now: he is not my son. Can't he get out of my house? Out of my house and to hell! If only he would die like a dog! I haven't got any children – I never had any. I haven't got a wife. I don't know this bastard. Get out of my house, you aren't my son, do you hear? You aren't my son!'

He carried on like this for a long time. I was stunned by the barrage of abuse. Finally he jumped on me like a possessed man, beat me up and threw me out. The others looked on. My aunt took me in for the night and comforted me. She did not try to hide her pleasure at my story. That night I found her to be much more my father's sister than my aunt. The night I spent there was an endless nightmare of tears, screams and 'snakes' heads'.

Monsieur Capel often kissed his wife on the mouth in front of us. I could see Father's heavy prick bulging in his trousers every time. My head swam. Mi blushed and disappeared into the back of the hut. They needed us there to stimulate them.

One morning I made a heap of gadgets out of planks for Nicole, to earn a glipse of her sex. I cut my finger with the saw and scraped another with the hammer. I caught my breath. Nicole's sex was sweet to the sight and covered with downy fair hair. Nothing like our women's permanently shaven genitals. I begged her to let me touch it but she said no.

'Your hands are dirty and anyway you only said "see" and you've seen!'

She pulled up her knickers and let her dress fall back into place.

'Let me touch it or kiss it and I'll show you mine!'

She burst out laughing.

'If you want me to look at yours you'll have to make me something else, and if you want to touch mine you'll have to invent something really ingenious for me.'

I wasn't a genius.

I was in my nightmare, walking. Suddenly father stopped shouting. He was waist-deep in the freezing water of Titahcen, pale-faced and dark-eyed, weeping waxen tears. The water was red – redder than blood. It was night. Ants were biting his chest and head. More and more of them and they were blacker and blacker, tearing the poisoned flesh and skittering away with shreds of meat. Others followed with hideous regularity, took their bit of poisoned flesh or bone and vanished as if by magic into the dark.

Father soon lost his own appearance. He looked more like

a scarecrow than a mangy dog. But the comparison immediately seemed absurd for he really did not resemble either. He was himself: a ruin with a dog's head. His *tarbouche* was at the mercy of the waves, sometimes washing up against a reef.

I felt sick, stepped back, and trod in something wet. Wet and warm. Unthinking, I twisted round and was startled to find my foot in a pool of blood. I wanted to pull it out of the horrible mess but could not free myself. I kept trying and lost my balance, fell into the red pool and started thrashing about. I was in a panic and was only sinking deeper. I saw the bushes on the shore were rustling. I turned to look: a giant ant was bearing down on me. It took my shirt tail in its jaws and easily pulled me free. I was out of danger but scared the ants would eat me too. Just then that prospect was preferable to the blood pool. I was amazed and moved when the animal withdrew, glancing back at me affectionately. For a moment I was speechless. Then I remembered I had been witnessing a tragedy much more terrible than my own. I turned again, and was shaken at the sight.

Si H'mad was sure the French were to blame for what had happened to us all. I did not understand his logic, but then he was hardly logical. He said once:

'I don't know how to explain this to you. It is hard for me, you understand. No one ever lifted a finger to teach me how to explain what happens in life. I'm an ass, according to "them". Perhaps it's true. But I do have one idea – no, it's a conviction! Everything bad that happens to us is their fault – yes, it's their fault. I would swear it on the Koran. I said so one day to your father. He was not pleased. You know what his answer was? . . .'

Father was completely covered by the tide of ants. His right hand still held a candle (now extinguished) and was thickly

111

coated with wax, and his eyes floated on the red surface like two burnt corks. I sprang round to run away and glimpsed Mi through the dense fog rising from the surface. She was squatting with a skimmer in her hand, intently gathering the slivers of flesh that the insects missed. She put each bit she fished out on her right, and tried to piece Father together from the shreds. I was surprised to see how pointlessly persistent she was.

The eyes were still afloat: the only part of his body the animals had spared. And those black eyes glared at me with hatred. They went on floating for a long time, then burst like soap bubbles and left a strong smell.

A deafening roar welled up from the depths of the spring. It grew louder – the walls and ground were shaking. A blinding flash, and there was Aïcha Qandischa in her goatskin shoes bursting from the impenetrable depths of inky redness, her chains clashing infernally and beams of light shooting from her eyes. Mi leaped up, tossed the skimmer aside, seized the unformed flesh-skeleton of father, clasped it to her bare breast and ran away as fast as she could. In her mad rush she did not notice that bits of flesh were dropping off. Aïcha Qandischa's fiery eyes rolled in her bovine head as she moved majestically towards the swarming ants that were scattering, jostling and stumbling over father's remains. Aïcha Qandischa leaned forward so that her heavy breasts floated on the water; she was spitting smoke and fire. The poor little insects were burned alive.

Before telling me what father's answer had been Si H'mad took a hot loaf out of the oven, broke it with his thumb and gave me a piece.

'He always seemed an odd one to me. His behaviour went against our truths. He insisted on seeing the French as supermen here to help and civilize us. He was not pleased. Well, he said:

"You don't understand anything about anything. Those

112

men you detest are our masters because they are a thousand times better than us. They know everything: they are strong, intelligent, honest, and always sincere. Open your eyes and see what they do for us – educating our children in their schools, giving Moroccans work in their factories, building road and dams in the countryside. They are thinking of our future and our kids' futures. They protect us from foreign invaders. At Christmas they give the beggars presents and our children sweets and new clothes. They teach good manners and tell us about their civilization. Do you know what this means? Don't you understand they are working for the good of all Moroccans?" '

The sky was so dark I could hardly see my hand in front of my face. Suddenly it was silent as death. I was horrified to see a great cloud lifting from the water. Qandischa held out her arms and Father was resurrected from the cloud. He looked sickly and some parts of his body were torn away – the scraps that Mi had gathered. Qandischa took the 'body' in her arms and gave it a terrible kiss. The body spun round and I saw two black holes where the eyes should have been. The rotting corpse stepped uncertainly forward, stumbled on a stone, fell heavily and sank without trace. I was astonished and horrified. I could bear no more and looked away. Through the transparent darkness I glimpsed a black stain on the flagstones around Titahcen. I went over and found my aunt sitting on the ground, naked as a joint of meat, her sex gaping, hair bristling, breasts scratched and bleeding, eyes revealing sin and perversion. She was holding a black cat between her legs and smiled as she stroked its head.

I shut my eyes tight and when I opened them again the sun was at its zenith. I was heavy as lead. My head ached and I was soaked with sweat. My aunt was there with her cat clutched in her lap, stroking it ceaselessly. She put a clammy hand on my forehead and told me it was late. I no longer understood what was going on. I was alone in my anguish, alone in my nightmare and madness, and now I was feverish and trembling under the blanket. I stared at my aunt and watched her inhuman eyes flicker with satisfaction. She leaned forward and informed me sharply that my splendid father had sold everything for a song. He had certainly gone mad and I must be his punishment.

Paths of fear yawned before me and closed again, as if shutting me in a cell. Barriers crowded in and cast shadows on the future.

When Mi returned from her trip she realized what a dreadful mistake she had made. In her eyes I alone was responsible for what had happened and she heaped abuse on me. It was quite clear I was solely and utterly to blame because I had done nothing to prevent the disaster. There was no doubt that I, as the man in the house, should have worked a miracle and kept things as they were. Yet all I had done was hide like a coward at my aunt's. I was beyond forgiveness; I knew it and it was not hidden from me.

I was condemned to universal contempt and indifference. Nobody understood that our disaster was a burden on my young back. It was easy for Mi to sow seeds of doubt and guilt in me. My responsibility was no longer a duty to be shouldered but a debt that had to be paid off.

'You are responsible for our tragedy!' They said it so often that I eventually believed I was actually guilty. They grumbled and pounced on me whenever I was late or opened my mouth; I was savagely attacked over single words – little words they would dissect and grind down to powder. So my little word uttered in all innocence and with no ulterior motive, became suspect, huge and deformed. It rained abuse. That is why I never understood anything that happened to us. I came to hate all my weaknesses.

I was convinced it was true. They had made me doubt my very identity. The whole family's behaviour reinforced these doubts: Father's rejection, Mi's indifference and the others' silence thickened and intensified them. It was hell. I had become the 'flood-child'. I was called that over and again at home. They had found me as they might a rusty jam-tin or a worm-eaten log.

Si H'mad took another loaf out of the oven and examined it before he tossed it to me. He went on in the same even voice:

'Obviously I didn't accept anything he said. He was just quoting their rubbish, and I wanted him to see that. I wanted to explain but it was too much for me. And then, he was obstinate. Yet he knew what I thought, like he knew that I didn't agree with the things he said. But he was sure of it himself and that is where you come in. One day I tried to explain again, and he treated me like a lunatic, a reactionary and a saboteur:

"Listen here, you're getting up my arse with your stories! You're an ignorant fool, so all you can do is hate. The sick man always wants the whole world to be sick with him. What have they done to *you*? You can't stand them because you're afraid to get near them and love them. You can't stand them because you don't *under*stand them. You can't be like them. You are pathetic and you know you're insignificant beside them. Life and Progress: that's what they are. You should be thanking them for their kindness and the day will come when you'll admit how right I was – when the others will admit it, when history will admit it. . ."'

Our elders vividly remembered the floods of the forties. They had scarred them so cruelly that they still related everything to those events when they wanted to establish a date.

'I went to Mecca two years before the floods.'

'Zoubida was born during the floods.'

Locusts, ration-books for bread and sugar, floods, drought. . . our points of reference in a painful existence. By talking so often about their tragedy, our parents passed some

115

of it on to us. The old people's heroism, patience, courage and hardiness rolled up its sleeves and came forward to shake our hands. Our parents were patient and brave, it could not be denied. Everyone was impressed, except me.

The story of the floods inspired jokes at my expense. No longer 'Son of Honey', I was the 'flood-child'. Or more explicitly I was nobody's child, certainly not Mi's and Father's. A bastard, perhaps? I was the nothing child, a useless mouth to feed against the bad days ahead. And the bad days came soon enough. Being a slave, I had to believe my inferiority was legitimate and live out my misfortune as a matter of course. The slave must have no sense of his own personality: that would make him uncontrollable; he must remain a slave to duty and gratitude for ever. Yet Mi had never treated me like a bastard. Life certainly did not cherish me, and still less did the people who opened my way into the desert of torment and hostility. And what if I really was the 'flood-child'?

I held the scorching bread for a second and put it on the plank. Si H'mad's bread gave me a warm feeling that I liked very much. He was smoking a *chqaf* of *kif* between batches and drinking the *dekka* that waited patiently in the black teapot. He continued:

'I wanted him to understand and accept that we were different from them. Understand how they were really depriving us of everything. We were abandoning our customs, our traditions, our pride, our beliefs, our religion – for a strange, alien civilization. You yourself, what have *you* learned at school? The story of Joan of Arc, *The Three Musketeers*, French geography, Christmas, *Monsieur Séguin's Goat*, Christian morality and charity. . . Six hours of French a day against one hour a week for Arabic. And what Arabic it is! You don't know if you are Arabs or Europeans. And you're neither. They've lost your voices for you. You are the children *they* want you to be, puppets strung between dreams and uncertainty. . .'

He paused.

'What language are we speaking now? What *is* this language we use? It's not Arabic any more but isn't French either. We've lost our dialect. I'm ashamed when I speak – I have to use words like tabla, sandala, traboublik, botagaz, carrossa, bichklit, jarda, camiou, t'rane, tomobile, ch'mane diffre, radiou, t'ractour. . . What *is* this language? I'm ashamed of speaking it and even more ashamed that imported, deformed words have been nailed for ever on to our language. Very often I can't find any equivalents in our own language, which has been deliberately neglected. This is real impoverishment and it's the source of all our problems. "They" murdered our language and destroyed our culture and what have they put in their place? A void. . . Boy, your father imitated them blindly. Now they have gone and he doesn't know where he is: he's completely lost. We were chatting once with friends about the state of the country. M'barek Bouchlaghem (the one with the moustache) suggested he join the *Istiqlal* party, like the rest of us. Well now! This will amaze you. I say again, he wasn't normal. . .'

Doubt is a terrible thing. I had once taken a secret look at the family papers. There I was – my entry among the others, like a sin. Why did they keep rejecting me?

In my presence eyes became blank, smiles became scowls, laughter warped into animal cries and words into grunts. I could read only indifference, aggression or contempt on the faces around me. I seemed to represent the others' fate, and it is quite possible not to like your own fate. They rejected and spurned me but they did not chase me away: I was indispensable to the expression of their hostility.

Bitterly, I realized I would have to stay a child all my life. More than that: a child to be beaten, insulted, and used as a pack-mule. In other people's eyes I was a child and must remain one so they could destroy me more easily. I had no right to grow up. My resignation and cowardice drove me to lose my own life among other lives, and live entirely confined in a narrow sphere. It was the beginning of my descent into hell.

As I watched Si H'mad I thought that for someone who had never set foot in a school, he knew a lot of things. Anyway, I was always sure you never learned anything about life at school. Si H'mad continued:

'For us the *Istiqlal* was the way to salvation. Your father didn't want to believe it. The nazarenes had hypnotized and bewitched him. He was purple with fury. He jumped up, his eyes bright with sin and hate, and said:

"You've never understood anything! You are incapable of charity, love and gratitude. You're all ungrateful! And racists. The *Istiqlal!* What's this shit politics that they're stuffing up your arses? Believe me, I understand people better than you. Do you think the *Istiqlal* will change our situation in the slightest? You're making a mistake. These proclamations, all this activity throughout the country – they are doing it for themselves to exploit us for their own ends. Open your eyes a crack! It's not so hard to understand. It's almost incredible. Who *are* these people who decided to set up this party for us? – They are *Fassis*, the leading citizens in the country. And a *Fassi* is like a Jew: not to be trusted. In the real fighting, in the mountains, in the *Jihad*, there are Arabs and *Chleuhs*. In the shadows the *Fassis* are in command, getting the country ready for their children studying in Europe who won't be back before independence. Then they will be the officers and put themselves in charge. The nazarenes you detest so much told me this, and I understand. Now you understand too!"'

My family was rocked by the turn of events. They had to be spared as much as possible. Now, irrevocably, I was their father and their freak son, a victim of others' madness and misery, shackled to daily anxiety; their dark-eyed phantom husband bringing betrayal and crime; their unworthy brother.

118

Fate had marked me out. I was full of secret loathing for the kingdom of the living and wondered if death could free me. I remember one day:

The tombs in the little cemetery were eager for our departure. Messaouda's mortal remains were there. I pictured them as plump: the flesh that had been bruised by the adults' frenzy was now the worms' luckless prey. Her soul was soon forgotten in the turmoil of consciences. Azrou sealed itself up again and its people sank passively into the frozen night. I realized that nothing, not even death, could jerk them out of their rut. The neighbours' dog barked in the cold night. Its bark splintered against the immensity of our silence. Who were we? We did not even know which way to turn, yet were condemned to walk beyond our suffering.

I picked up the history of the *Istiqlal* by word of mouth. It was a political party formed by one Allal El Fassi, who apparently played a leading role in Morocco's independence. Almost all Moroccans joined the party and were united in the struggle. Every week the members met secretly at one of their houses to discuss the state of the country and make donations to the party. During the feast of *Aïd el Kebir* people gave their sheeps' stomachs and fleeces. Mi burned her party receipts and card after independence.

Si H'mad stoked the oven with a few logs before going on:

'Your father and M'barek very nearly had a fight. Nobody could understand Driss. The others began to distrust him. He was a danger to us and the party. Everybody avoided him. Your mother asked me to enrol her secretly. He would have repudiated her if he'd known. A brave woman, your mother. Her life was hell: a patriot living with a traitor. Yes, no less than a traitor! He wouldn't understand "they" were doing everything for themselves. Roads, schools, buildings – they were using us to exploit our resources all the more easily. The *Istiqlal* was our guiding light and he preferred eternal darkness. Then M'barek grabbed him one day, during a violent demon-

119

stration and made him shout "Long live Sultan Sidi Mohammed ben Youssef!" M'barek had an axe and would certainly
have killed him if he hadn't done it. . . Back home I told him,
"Stop it! You're obsessed with the French. You could easily
get yourself killed. Watch out! I don't understand why you'd
rather be ruled by foreigners. You really must be mad. If what
just happened ever happens again, you had better pray for
your soul. . .'"

God the Father sent us to rot at the edge of Essaouira. We
were banished, torn from the stony soil that shaped our
memories. Scraps of our childhood stuck to the rocks and
mixed with the dust in the streets. We took the big stove with
us to warm our misery; but it wouldn't work, ever again. The
copper mortar and leather bellows also joined us in exile. Mi
had broken my go-cart, thrown away my hoop and sold my
bag of marbles to Issa the pedlar. I did not need them any
more: I was a man. The bloodstains on the white sheets were
in mourning. Mi was sure of it. She was determined to take
the filth of years with her. She was deeply attached to those
sheets. They exuded a smell of sperm and the past, and she
would never have any others. It was a difficult world; we had
to get used to it.
    The desert shores of our new destiny stuck to Mi's dull eyes.
She gazed at time flowing, but not passing for us. We were
not used to change. Our misfortune was inscribed on the line
of time. God willed it: God is generous!
    I remember one day: Mi, caught up in her *djellaba* and her
tears, still pursuing the dream of an avenging miracle. She
examined her silk scarf every morning. The knot was still
tightly tied. She waited a long time – then finally let go, and
sank.

Si H'mad took endless pains to explain. I was young and he
could not find the words to persuade me of his good faith. I

120

did understand some things, though plenty of others remained obscure; but I knew he was sincere and took him at his word.

A long time after independence, Nicolas (pronounced Nicoula) set his dogs on us when we were 'stealing' our cherries, pears, peaches and apples from him. This middle-aged colonist with rings on his fingers still cultivated the huge farm which no longer belonged to him. He had occupied it and kept on farming it just for himself. He had trained his dogs to go for Moroccans. We were all scared of them and him.

His dogs took us by surprise one afternoon under a cherry tree. T'hami was perching in the branches, tossing down the fruit. We could dash for it but T'hami had not dared to jump and was stuck up the tree. When we were out of reach the dogs turned back to the tree to wait for T'hami to come down and tear him to shreds. We were behind the barbed wire, chanting the Yassine and wailing.

'Nicoula' ran up, gun over his shoulder. He stroked his dogs and kissed them on their muzzles, then fired twice into the branches just wide of T'hami. We saw a thread of urine run down the trunk and spread on to the ground. 'Nicoula' had food brought for the dogs, since they were going to spend the night under the tree.

Allal was limping. His calf was bleeding; one of the dogs had bitten him. Ben Smimi urinated on the wound to disinfect it, and to stop the bleeding we sprinkled it with earth finely shifted through our fingers. Then we covered it with a leaf and bound it up with a rag. That was how we usually treated our wounds when we were protected by the Great Civilized Nation.

T'hami took to his bed a few months later. He was visibly dwindling away. His parents brought a *taleb* to the house who wrote an amulet for him. For that honourable quack there was no doubt about it: the child was 'possessed by *djinnoun*'. He recommended them to take the boy to Moulay Brahim. His health still did not improve. T'hami died on their return from the Siyed. One Friday in autumn. His father used to say pathetically: 'My son was lucky – he died on a Friday!'

121

We three knew the real cause of his death. Just as we three knew the secret of the hatred we felt for the colonist.

I did have the courage to tell Si H'mad everything. He laughed and said:

'Nicoula, Monsieur Capel, Monsieur Noble – they are all the same: an army of occupation. . .' The memory of Monsieur Noble instantly sprang to mind.

Monsieur Noble was head of the 'European School' (which became the 'Muslim School' after independence) and was the model of the perfect colonist. He learned Arabic and even a few passages of the Koran. We all admired the ardour, pride and great-heartedness of that conscientious settler. We used to swear by his name. Everyone asked his advice about everything.

He had been kept on, irreplaceable and immortal, after independence. School was hardly conceivable without him. Who else could have run the place so well? The *medersa* in anybody else's hands? – It was not to be thought of, especially if the hands might belong to some native or other. As permanent head of the school he had 'built on our backs', he was feared and respected.

To the townspeople his eventual departure was a catastrophe. They organized a great farewell ceremony for the occasion and everyone praised his integrity, seriousness, devotion and patience through all those years in Azrou.

The ceremony ended with a presentation. The people gave him as keepsakes a large carpet from the Middle Atlas and a magnificent silver salver. Then they wept at fate's harshness.

A few days later it was noticed – but too late – that he had taken the school's state grant with him as well as the carpet and salver.

Monsieur Noble: a wise and civilized man!

Father was strutting triumphantly on top of the hill. He had 'the filth of the world', and acquired pubescent wives with ease. Life smiled on him, as it smiled on all dogs of his kind.

122

Blood still flowed for him and mourned behind white sheets. That was his fate!

Although everything was against us, Mi kept telling us to hope: God would sort everything out somehow or other. And how well he had done so far! – When I was younger Lalla Zahra, the fortune-teller, had foreseen a better future for me:

'I see him,' she said to Mi, 'sitting behind a big desk. An important position with the *Maghzen*. . . Lots of money. He will go far in life. A good sign: the child is bright. . . Fine, a few problems, but soon free! A long illness, may God keep him from the eyes of the children of the adulteress. He'll leave home in seven days, seven weeks, seven months or seven years – I can't be more exact. What else do I see? – Women! Here's one. What next, Lalla? No, they are separating – look at the cards yourself! Just as well, she wasn't right for him. A blue-eyed Roumia. God keep him from the children of the adulteress! Beware of the women, Lalla! Here's another. . . marriage. . . children. . .'

Mi went white and almost fainted. The fortune-teller saw and swiftly took her chance:

'Don't worry, Lalla, I've got what you need to make your worries go away. Come and see me again next Friday. The props are a bit expensive. I know you are generous and I'm sure we can agree a price. . . Don't forget a lock of his hair and some nail parings. . .'

Mi kissed the good woman and gave her fifty centimes and some sugar. Back home she heaped abuse on me for my prophesied girlfriends. After that I lived only for the future meeting with my blue-eyed French girl.

One day I overheard a conversation between Father and Si H'mad, who had come to say he deplored Father's decision to leave and wanted him to put an end to his madness.

'You'll be sorry one day! You have children, you are known here, you have work and a house, your wife is good and meek, "may God make this house fruitful!" What are you looking

123

for anywhere else? Trouble is what you'll find, make no mistake!'

'That's my business, "A Si H'mad"! You can have her if you admire her so much. An ignorant, neurotic, old-fashioned woman – that's all she is.'

'But what do you have to complain about?'

'I'll tell you, as you're asking. You know she refuses to sleep with me? – and when she does give her consent, it must be as normal as possible: the usual routine, no more! Never during the day. At night – only at night and with the light out. Isn't that old-fashioned?'

'I don't understand you. Our parents taught us to respect ourselves and our wives. How could respect survive between you if she was ready to be your whore?'

'So the French women who are willing to satisfy their husbands' every desire are whores? They do it as a matter of course and in all simplicity. . .'

'In all simplicity but shamelessly too. You have just admitted your flaw, Si Driss: you want to imitate them in everything. You've got to admit it's not possible.'

'You can't understand! The age of the women's room is over. Times have changed and we must change too. What use to me is a women I can't be in love with, a woman I don't feel anything for any more?'

'They have led you astray, there's no doubt about it. I will pray to the All Powerful to lead you back to the right path. It isn't a wife you need, but a bitch!'

'No, "A Si H'mad"! All I'm looking for is a simple uncomplicated wife, a wife who will make love to me without being ashamed, undress in front of me without blushing and share my pleasure – who will love me, that's what!'

'One day you'll regret this moment's madness. It's our way to behave like human beings, not animals. You made the rash mistake of getting too near them and you caught their "syphilization". That is *their* way of life – not ours.'

'It's a great pity you do not know them properly. You don't like them because the others have set you against them – you never liked them. But I'll always say that living with them was very good. They were fine people: simple and uncomplicated. I understand why you are worried. . .'

'And I understand why you worship them. You are incapable of keeping your own character. You worship them because you could sleep with the wife in full view of her husband. And you claim that's evolution and progress. You worship them because they let you forget your own condition. You have lost everything! Go back to God and beg his forgiveness. . .'

I forget how the meeting ended, but I do remember crying as I listened behind the door.

Ba Benaïssa the minced-meat seller always said I was 'God's child'. I did not know what he meant.

'I'm Mi's child!' I shouted indignantly. Then he laughed in sympathy, gave me a friendly tap on the shoulder and said:

'We are all God's children, my boy. Happy are they who fear him and are gathered into his Kingdom!'

'I know that, Ba Benaïssa, but I'm Mi's child and that is enough for me. I don't want to be anybody else's child just now!'

I never suspected that good-humoured laughter foretold my future. I was the nest-egg child saved for bad days ahead.

Sometimes Mi curbed her bad temper but then, encouraged by my sisters, it was soon replaced by indifference. I did not understand why her mood darkened whenever she discovered I had been out with a girl. She used all her power to dissuade me from persisting in my folly. To her everything I did was folly. No girl was worthy of me. When I took no notice she issued her final ultimatum: 'Curse on the one hand, blessing on the other: it is your choice!' I should stay away from the female son-stealers. She was extremely possessive and she sifted through my little relationships, which were often cut short by gossip.

Once in his life, Father had the courage or recklessness to

break loose and escape, to rediscover himself somewhere else. A huge black rat lay in wait on the pavement. It pounced like a starving tiger, tore off a chunk of flesh and vanished into the thick fog. That had not stopped Father in his headlong race to the whores and innocent young girls.

Father was stupid and wicked, and it was some consolation to know that. If what Grandmother said about wickedness and lying was true, Father would soon be turned into an animal for treating us so badly. Such is God's will!

God – would God strike him down? Was God watching our misery? He had so many other important things to do. Urgent things too. We waited endlessly for justice and Mi went on crying. Patience built a nest between her withered breasts. And I had no rights but silence. I braced myself by remembering that I would have my reward once day in the hereafter (that is, in hell). Mi often said that God rewarded the faithful. I was definitely not one of them, and destiny had never given me anything for nothing.

Si H'mad was right. The importance of his words was dawning on me: the nazarenes had infected father with their madness and mediocrity. Si H'mad was certainly right; the protectors were not all as sincere as they claimed to be. After they left Azrou, Si H'mad declared:

'Look what they leave us! Emptiness, a deep abyss and the whole town to be rebuilt. A few miles of broken road which they used to move our minerals, phosphates and animal-skins, a few houses they lived in and we built. Slaughterhouse-schools where they murdered our culture and standards. . . What else have they left? A void, nothing but a void! Even if they *have* left us Madame Karabourou, that relic of France. . .'

The last baby that Mi lost, one winter's morning, woke me one night and gazed at me with baby's eyes. He was angelically beautiful and had a warm, trustful expression. I gave him a brotherly smile back. He asked:

126

'Brother, who are you?'

'I'm your brother.'

'I know, but what else?'

'I'm the son of Driss and Mi. I'm the punishment for their n. I'm sorrow, I'm the abandoned mistake.'

'You're called Abdelhak, son of Driss?'

'That's my name.'

'I don't have a name.'

'So what do you want?'

'Nothing. I don't want anything – anything I can hope to have.'

'Tell me about the women and how they do it where you are. . .'

Everyone in Azrou knew Madame Karabourou. She had settled with a husband who did not last long there. She was sole tenant of a vast property which we were forbidden to dirty with our feet. Madame Karabourou was not her real name: the kids called her that because she was so ugly. She was a horrible woman, always dressed in black and never leaving her house. No one knew how or why she kept herself alive. She was mere skin and bone. The day after independence, her own kin had not bothered to encumber themselves with a French skeleton whose days plainly were numbered. She had mysteriously defied time. Whenever we went near her house she started screaming and waving her broom:

'Help! Police! Catch those thieves! Catch those devils, put them in prison! Help! Lock them up! Shoot them! Why is our Morocco rotten with tramps and savages?. . .'

Then we lined up at the edge of her property and chanted in chorus, clapping our hands, 'Ma-dame-Kara-bourou-give-me-*niqui*. . . Ma-dame-Kara. . .' A grown-up usually intervened with stones and sent us packing.

In my dream, the image of my stillborn brother filled my

127

memory. I told him so, to cheer him up.

'Our women are a disgrace. Mi is desperate. We're acting out a tragedy where the characters die of hate rather than love. Our tragedy is inside us. We carry our misunderstanding within us, as we have for thousands of years. Our ancestors were already cloistering the women and gelding the children. Our own fathers tore our virgin mothers and froze their ripening youth. Blood flowed and still flows between the virgins', the women's and the children's legs. And sometimes down the very street: the red liquid is displayed, borne in triumph on a dish. It's the blood of the eternal wound and of defilement. Hadda still washes the stained clothes. She still sweeps. She wakes at six every morning summer and winter. She still yields to One-Eye's joyless lust, injecting his male poison in the usual silence and secrecy. Mi has been repudiated yet still wears the veil. She still scrapes along the walls when she's out and never dares look at a man. When she talks to one she keeps her eyes on the ground and calls him *Sidi*. Mi no longer has a husband. She has sealed herself away from the male sex. She weeps as before. She is nostalgic for tears – can't live without them – has to cry to know she exists. She has to suffer a little too. The chains of the past have rusted on her wrists. Mi the woman-animal is chained to yesterday and cannot live any other way. The male is the lion: he's the one who speaks, commands, belches and farts in the house like bad weather. He is scared of his wife but knows her weakness. He crushes and fucks her, educates her in submission. *That* is what he's proud of. From then on, he simply perpetuates her frailty to keep himself on top.

'When Mi was abandoned she wept, threatened and swore – she didn't get a hammer and smash his skull as he deserved. Should she not have found a knife, opened his stomach, and given us his guts to eat? Or wouldn't she have done better to amputate his prick and throw it to the dogs in the street? Then he wouldn't have felt the slightest desire to go anywhere else. She did not do any of those things.'

128

Si H'mad once asked me if I knew the story of Itto. I shook my head and felt ashamed. He smiled kindly and delivered a very unpleasant sermon:

'"They" only taught you about Christmas and Easter. They taught you the history and geography of Mother France, which you now know perfectly, but not those of your own country. That's the sum of what they taught you in their famous schools: only things that displace you from your own reality. Don't you think it's terrible? It is part of their "politics of exploitation". Pretentious snobs! They thought the earth turned around them and we were frightened of them through superstition. But it is our fault: when all is said, we sold them our country ourselves. And you aren't doing anything to fight off that lethargy. You enjoy superficial things and don't even seem to want to learn. You aren't all that interested in your country or your own lives. You don't ever search, don't ever question anything. What a generation! Yours is the generation of the end of the world. . .'

I dared not interrupt to ask for the story of Itto. I knew he would come to it sooner or later.

'Look what they've done to the descendants of Tarik ben Ziyad, Mahdi ben Toumert, Youssef ben Tachfine, Moulay Ismaïl – those snail-gobblers have forgotten history, forgotten our glorious past. What an age this is! We belong to God and will return to him. . .'

Si H'mad was beside himself. I had never seen him in such a state. He had his reasons.

'They did all they could to split father from son, wife from husband, man from his brother and his land. They made a Berber College to set the *Chleuhs* against the Arabs. Segregation and racism between two men of the same blood and name. They stuck their fingers up their own arses with their famous Berber *tahir* – *that* conspiracy will drag us all into bloodshed. Never have the Moroccans felt so united! Let them remember! And remember the massacres too – Juin, Pétain, Lyautey, Guillaume and all their bloodsoaked victories! Let them remember! I don't understand why those people wanted to hurt us. Thousands of Moroccans were wiped out for a few cursed buckets of minerals. . .'

His anger was inflated but I knew Si H'mad's heart was in the right place. He did not hate anybody. They used to say that Moroccans cannot hate (I mean, not hate to the point of murder). They only kill when they must, in legitimate defence. Beware their fury! Si H'mad began the famous history of Itto:

'It was an age when women existed. They will tell you that Itto is a mythical figure. Itto – a myth! They have wreathed a halo of mystery around her. The Benis M'guild and the Benis M'tir of the Middle Atlas will tell you that. Itto certainly lived and she was a millstone round the necks of the Foreign Legion. There aren't any women like her nowadays. She travelled the region alone, a living communication link between the different resistance groups. A woman like no other. The devils finally exhausted her courage and daring. Itto was not history to them, and history only keeps what it is given: they make and unmake their famous history as they please. History: better not to speak of it. They murdered our own. . .'

In his distraction Si H'mad had forgotten to take his loaves out of the oven. The first one he rescued was black. Si H'mad was very proud of his reputation and I was sorry for him:

'Shit! What a mess! Damn their mothers' faith! Look at that – even when they've gone they still hurt us. What a curse. They can keep God! They can keep God! . . .'

Si H'mad was winding up to give me a lengthy talk on the period of the protectorate. I sensed it coming and began to be sorry I had come that day. I was tired.

The image of the stillborn still filled my memory. I continued:

'We're living in an age which can't bear delicacy. Love, sincerity, friendship and charity are all rotting in dustbins. There is only room in our lives for profiteering and corruption.

'With us, men lie, women try, children die. It is one of our laws of nature: the law of inequality and injustice. Look at the dawning day: it is grey, sin-coloured, and the sun is bitter yellow. Do you know why you died? Mi was alone in her confinement as usual, in a cold bedroom one winter's morning. It was snowing. The walls and roof dripped and Mi, flat out like a wounded dog, was groaning, screaming, twisting. . . Got up to knead the dough. . . make the meal. . . Hafid and I were desperate. She bit her lips and wept. . . went back to bed. We fidgeted about in the room. . . helped her as best we could. . . wept. She bit herself like a dog with a crushed tail. It was snowing, snowing. The sheepskin waited for you with its usual patience. Her black-ringed eyes wept hailstones. . . Took the bucket of lime and washed down the wall. People would be coming, the wall must be clean, a matter of principle. The icy cold pierced our bones, steeled the sheepskin. . . She was weeping, shouting. Hafid wept and trembled. Mi was alone in her pain. . . still weeping. The water wasn't heating on the ashy stove. She groaned. . . screamed. The sheepskin was waiting, unmoved. . . She twisted, looked like a rutting horse. . . She was praying to the one who was still deaf to her calls. . . I was trembling in my helplessness. . . A crow landed on the window ledge – evil against the white background. . . Shouting and yelling, grasping anything in reach, biting her hand like a starving beast and blood running, a river of blood. . . Skin flushed and I saw you coming into the world, like every other baby except you were cold. . . didn't cry. I remember. . . you didn't even see the world you entered. Blackness. You did not make a sound. . .

'Mi cut the birth-cord and wrapped you in a white sheet she had ready. She wiped herself and got up to see to her tattered body. Hafid and I took the sheepskin to the river and washed it. The water turned red.

'Father came home a few hours later, picked you up and took you to the cemetery. We followed him with dignity. I had a pick, Hafid a shovel. He named you as he put you in your hole: Mustapha.'

Si H'mad smoked a *sebsi* and calmed down. I wondered how he would face his customers. He gave me some money and told me to buy thirteen loaves in the market. He would apologize to his customers for the substitution. I was gone for a few minutes and when I returned Si H'mad did not even stop to thank me. He motioned me to put the loaves on the trestles and continued his lecture:

'While murdering our culture and traditions they subtly set about destroying our religion. First they deported our Sultan. That was treason and the first attack on religion: we couldn't pray after that: in whose name would we be praying? Then they infiltrated the entire country with monasteries and convents. Here, the monks of Tioumliline worked cunningly to turn our children from the path of Islam. It was a well-organized conspiracy: a political, social and religious conspiracy. We really were in danger. And the French cancer spread, *aoulidi*. Your father for one, and plenty of others, alas! were led to damnation by them. . .'

All the children in Azrou knew Tioumliline. We went there every Sunday. As soon as we had finished stuffing ourselves at the nazarenes' 'dustbin' we stowed our treasures at home and went in small groups to the monastery through the forest of Sabbab. This path became dangerous later, when Toto Assou set up his gang. Toto was huge and tanned, with a cleft lip and boats instead of feet. He could never find shoes to fit so Hassan the shoemaker rigged up some leather sandals with soles cut from old car tyres.

Toto had lost his father when still little. His mother had no work and was past her youth. She began pimping with Touda to help raise the swarm of brats her husband had left her. Every morning Toto described the genitals, sperm and stifled moans:

'Yesterday your father had Daouya, my elder sister. It was almost midnight. I still wasn't asleep. There were other customers about. I was waiting for a free bed. Your father gave me a réal and asked me to buy him some dried figs. At midnight. My other brothers and sisters were asleep in a corner of the room. In another corner my mother was making mint-tea. That is a craze of your father's: drinking tea afterwards. I pretended to go out but came back straightaway. Your father's great bottom was rising and falling. He had covered Daouya's face with a towel. He only liked her vagina and her little breasts. The rest disgusted him. His arsehole opened and closed. I wanted to fuck it just to see how it reacted, but I didn't out of respect for his forty réals. My mother saw and passed me a bit of kitchen soap. I wanked on his arse. He started raving just before he shot his poison into my sister. What a bastard! Do you know what he said?'

'What?'

'"Ahh! O my beloved. O dear sister. O my life. Your vagina is a honey-pot. Ahh! Your breasts are paradise apples. Ahh! Ahhh! O my little bitch! O my negress! Ahhh! . . . Ahhhh! . . '. Come to me my whore! take me my slave! Ah! . . . Ahhh! . . . Ahhhhhhhhhh!"

'I wasn't so sad, because *that* night your father didn't thrash her with his belt before having her.'

After her confinement Mi put on her flame-red scarf. So Father was free to go to the Kechla to relieve his aching balls between indifferent, anonymous legs.

Lalla (for so our grandmother was called) arrived three days after your burial. The blood had been washed out of the sheep-skin but not out of my memory. Father picked up his tools, Mi went back to the kitchen, and life continued as before – without you. Sometimes I longed to be an idiot, not to think or feel any more. The smile hardened into a horrid grin and the line of time petrified it in our memories. The wall of our house became flat and dark once again. We live in an age of hate.

You passed unnoticed: one grief among other cries and tears. Mi had wept openly. Hafid too. Father merely muttered a prayer – no more – as he put you underground. You did well to go the way you did!

There has been no daylight since your burial, and death soaked into our lives.

Our 'fathers' bustled around us as soon as we arrived at Tioum-liline. First they distributed bread, sometimes with cheese or chocolate too. Then they gave us one or two rubber balls. Towards eleven o'clock they gathered us round a table and spoke for along time about a certain 'Jesus', whom we later realized was none other than the 'Issa' in the Koran. At first they claimed he was a prophet of the same rank as 'Sidna Mohammed'. Later, he turned into 'the Prophet', and he alone must fill our hearts and souls. In the same way they explained the advantages of Christianity and exposed the failings of Islam.

Some of us were convinced by this Christian nourishment and began to eat during Ramadan. They asked us to listen and trust in their good faith. We had to kiss the Bible before praying. Then we sat down to eat.

We live in an age of misery. Our fever at that time was black, and black our patience, black our thoughts and sighs. . . Not only are we living in an age of hatred, misery and blood; the real truth is, we are no longer alive at all.

We were passing through a long silence. It was so strong that only a miracle could have broken it: an earthquake, say, massive enough to rattle the bad consciences. The one that came some time after your death was so persuasive that Father fell sick. Surely God had a part in that. The men hurriedly reached for their prayer beads, unrolled their mats and became good Muslims. The poor and the beggars were briefly sheltered from need, and the lie was carved on waxen faces.

Toto's gang became a menace. There was a rape at Sabbab every week. Toto had spies, and the lovers were hardly settled under a tree when Toto and his gang appeared from nowhere, armed with sticks, faces masked with scarves. The gang sur-

134

rounded their prey and forced them to perform sexual contortions before they raped them. Toto was delighted when one of his victims happened to be someone who had slept with his sister or one of the girls working for his mother.

When game was in short supply, Toto sometimes put on his mother's *djellaba* and some khôl, veiled himself, and went to the *souq*. Where a simple *Chleuh* always fell into the trap. Faced with such danger our visits to Tioumliline stopped.

We missed the Fathers' bread, sweets and cheese, the *djellabas* and woollen jumpers they handed out when the first snow fell, and even the slices of ham they made us eat and the occasional mouthfuls of red wine.

The good sisters at Mismanhout, a little convent on the periphery of the Kechla, took devoted good care of our women.

We are living in a moment of transition between hypocrisy and doubt. Not even a month had passed before night descended again. The men hung up their beads, tossed the prayer mats aside, tore off their masks and showed themselves as they had always been – inhuman. They redoubled their ferocity towards their children and wives and recovered their own bestial – natural – behaviour.

God shut the little window that looked on to us and we wept for his floods, locusts, earthquakes and storms. Day after day the same relentless monotony, pretence, hypocrisy and hatred. Azrou became again the little hollow dead town, and the birds perished in the spring. I had had enough. I wanted to leave and I told Mi so. She scowled and her eyes shone with contempt.

Si H'mad was speaking. I was listening. I wondered why everyone took such pleasure in hurting me with their words, and knew that at the same time I had made all their languages my own. That disturbed me. For a moment I forgot Si H'mad and the battering of his speech:

'Your father was finished. The rest of us had hopes for the future. You know, the party leaders had pledged that life would be easier and more beautiful. They promised liberty, equality and justice. Can you understand what that meant? Me for example, I'd be able to take a rich man to court and win. Justice! – Do you understand? Your father did not believe it. That was his choice. He did not *want* to admit that we were exploited and that independence would restore our national pride and character. He was blinded by the nazarenes. He did not *want* to believe we could each have ten *dirhams* a day from our phosphates, without even working. Ten *dirhams* a day for every single Moroccan! It was our right, and that was what our leaders repeated the day I dragged him to one of our secret meetings. Back home he said:

"What rubbish! Where in the world do they give you money you haven't worked for? They will promise anything to make use of you. Wait and see what they do with you when we have independence! You'll see! God grant us long life so that you'll see! God grant us long life! . . ."

'Your father was incurable. He preferred a foreigner to profit from our wealth. I think he was a bit mad. He refused to understand. I did try again one day but he did not want to know. They had completely messed him up. Nothing to be done about it. He was lost for ever. When I got angry he listened carefully, but never said a word.

"Who are you working for?" I shouted one day. "Who are you burning up your years for? Who? Can you tell me that? – For foreigners who don't care about you or your work. What guarantees do we have? We work like dogs. We are their pack-animals and slaves. No freedom, no consideration. . . With independence we will be masters of this country, and it needs us. We shall work with dignity. A better life is round the corner. We shall have pensions for our retirement and social security. Our children will all be taught free in the *medersa*. They will be cared for, and we shall have family allowances for them. Enough to clothe them and let them live properly. Women who stay at home will have allowances too. We will be able to go on holiday. Our children will blossom – they will all become managers and make the nation prosper. Our lives will be easier and more beautiful. The government will build free housing for the poor, pull down the disgraceful shanties and put up splendid villas. We shall have cars and eat meat every day. No more oppression: we shall be free – free! We shall be happy, our children will be happy, even our dogs will be happy!"

'But your father was a small-minded man. He saw the sun and threw a blanket over it. Yet even the ones who didn't have much faith joined us – all except him. He let me talk on and on, then sneered and went away. . .'

My idea of leaving died the death almost immediately, killed by savage opposition.

'You have been a curse from the day you were born,' Mi burst out. 'You want to get out and leave us up to our ears in shit. It's too hard for idiots like you. The biggest nuts are always hollow. Think of Salah, Lalla Hnia's son, God bless him! He takes good care of his mother and five brothers and sisters. He never upsets his mother. And he even promised to send her to Mecca next year. He's a blessed child, not like you. Damn you! Go, and never let me hear your name again! I shall find work with the nazarenes to keep your brothers and sisters. Go! You're not my son any longer and I'm not your mother. Go! . . .'

I gulped back my idea, wiped my streaming face, and went to lie down in a corner. That night my eyelids were so heavy with despair that they would not shut. And in the other room – silence.

Next day, it was still night in Mi's mind. She would not look at me and now I was entitled to nothing but scorn and indifference from all sides. O if you knew, my brother! I ate alone; I was a monster now so they fed me on leftovers. They were determined to make my life worthless and I quickly had to accept their terms.

137

I still remember when the Capels left. It was the day after independence. The wife was weeping at the entrance to their villa. She had given my mother some of her short dresses and high-heeled shoes, and a box of make-up. It was another way of humiliating Mi. We were weeping (Father's orders). Men were busy moving furniture. Father was saying yet again that Monsieur Capel had sold his villa for next to nothing. He was weeping and helping to load the furniture. 'Why is the traitor weeping?' I wondered. 'Is it really because his neighbours are going away, or for the villa he could not get his hands on?' Some of each. And much more for my lady Capel. I had a grief of my own: the house had been built for Nicole and I could not bear to think of any other girl living there.

Monsieur Capel kissed father's wet cheeks and declared vengefully:

'Look how the Moroccans are rewarding us! They are throwing us out. How ungrateful they are. They wanted their independence and now they have it! And they can shove it up their arses! May they put it to good use, at least. I will be back in ten years to see what they made of it. They're making a terrible mistake, I tell you now. But what can I do? They don't understand anything at all – they're primitive, they're savages! . . .'

In his rage my lord Capel had forgotten that he too could die. But there was no reaction to the Frenchman's words, because we still felt inferior to him.

Mi was always immovable when it came to education. She never let me have my own way. In her eyes I was a man and she treated me accordingly. I was allowed no mistakes, no carelessness.

Eventually she accepted my independence. She was sure the bonds between us were stronger than bad luck, stronger than any other facts. She was opening a road to me, and she knew

138

the road would bring me back to her. Our relations returned to normal and we discovered the delight of simple generosity. So the family seized a few happy hours from life.

But I never forgot the last time Mi was angry with me.

'You think you are strong, you think you are clever, you think you are another Sidi Khlil. But really you are not worth anything in this world. You are nothing but a turd among all the other turds in this shit-heap. . .'

She had to be furious to speak so grossly. It happened one night when I had just missed supper. It must have been about eight o'clock. And it was the first time we had ever eaten so late. Mi needed an excuse to stamp on me and humiliate me. She had concocted one, and now she inflated it dramatically. I saw what she was doing quickly enough but wanted to know where it would lead.

'But it's only. . .'

Her answer was fast: she spat in my face. I did not dare raise my hand. My sight was blurred and all at once I was face to face with a stranger.

'So now he dares contradict me! He dares shout at the mother who carried him for nine months. You think you're getting hairs on your chest, you cocksparrow! You have been damned from the day you were born. What a damned age we live in! There is no shame, no respect any longer. "No fire without ash" – how true it is. O if only God would lead us into the light! . . .'

It was out of the question to explore Mi's anger any further. I shut up and went to my corner. That night, as so many others, I slept wide-eyed and hollow-bellied; for heaven, so they say, lies under a mother's feet.

The assault left its marks, but I always remember that woman's battle against a dark and dead-end life only with a sort of sadness: her endless tenacity was her flat refusal to let us destroy ourselves. That refusal makes her an extraordinary woman.

Mi, time's wound
and men's
like Messaouda
Azrou carved in rock
and faces too
Memories swept
by fate's waves
across the unforgiving emptiness of words
that sometimes take
intolerable steps
often dying
like monstrous reptiles

And speech rising from the ashes

'Abraham was not a Jew or a Christian. . .'
Nor was I a Jew or a Christian. Yet, in front of this heavy
face and absurd *tarbouche*, I wanted to be Jewish or Christian.
The night was freezing and the stove was cold. I struggled to
control the tremors of cold and rebellion shaking my body.
Father was speaking. He didn't bellow nowadays. He was no
longer dealing with a docile, fearful child, but a young man
ready to use his fists and hurt people. He knew it and was
very careful to keep me in check. He would not look at me.
I beat the iron; it was cold.

'To be frank, you don't mean anything to me any longer,
nor to the others. You made us live like dogs, but you would
have done better to deny yourself the pleasure. It would have
saved us so much sorrow. . .'
The iron was still cold.

'Abraham was not a Jew or a Christian. He wanted to

140

sacrifice his son. . .'

Father had clearly learned a thing or two since leaving us. He knew now that Abraham was neither Jewish nor Christian and it pleased him to repeat this as if to persuade me that our separation had put him back on a good footing. Yet there were still so many things between us that we had to get clear before dawn.

'Abraham. . .'

I attacked:

'Wasn't Jewish or Christian. So?'

The room was muggy. The cold trailed over the grey walls, across the cracked ceiling, over the damp earth floor. . . We were being watched from above his wooden bed by the great stag's head I had scraped clean and varnished long ago.

Father shifted his position and the bed creaked. The movement and the bed's noise reminded me of Mi and the long vigils when she retold the story of her life.

'You know I only sacrificed you all because I could not go on any longer. . .'

He was looking for excuses. I couldn't take that and decided to stop the lie in mid-flight. I was not going to let him convince me of his innocence, and was too impatient to hear him out.

'You're just a coward! Are you going to sacrifice the others as well? – the ones you had by your other wives, your innumerable other wives?'

He was not expecting that and was plainly embarrassed. I knew he would not answer and decided to make him bitterly regret the day he conceived me in my mother's womb.

I peeled off ten years of life and pictured myself again, minute before his tyranny. Now the roles were reversed: he was so small before my hatred that I pitied his insignificance. He was silent. I knew he would not answer so I decided to do it for him: he must be stopped from thinking.

'They will certainly share the same fate – the street! It was another way of humiliating us: multiplying your spawn so we would always be bumping into you on every street corner. And that's what you call tradition! How could they let some-

141

one your age multiply his sexual crimes legally by breeding victims he would never be able to look after properly, children doomed to be orphans from birth to the day they die? — And in between they learn to grow old and mad by watching your blank face and crumpled memories. Every day you age a thousand years, and every day you kill them a little more. . .'

He was still silent. My feet were frozen and my spine prickled with disgust. The lamp flickered and immediately – I don't know why – made me think of an earthquake. I suddenly felt sick. Would God be so cunning as to bring us together in a disaster? I dismissed the possibility; pigs must die alone. He opened his mouth and spoke more lies:

'You are my son! It is your right of course to judge me harshly after what happened, and spit in my face. . .'

I spat on the ground. The rasping noise cut across Father's words. He looked at my spit for a second, then up again. I could not bear his tired eyes, stripping me naked. I stared at the spit and knew I had just let myself down. I attacked before he could sense my confusion:

'I am *not* your son! And I am not here to judge you – that has already been done. I am here to condemn you because I don't find any mitigating circumstances. . . So stop calling me your son! You always treated me like a bastard in the past. You are forgetting I'm the "flood-child".'

Like the spitting, my voice betrayed me. The change in my tone was not lost on him. He tried again to draw me into the trap that I had managed to avoid so far.

'Ibrahim El Khalil was not. . .'

That refrain was maddening. He was pretty shrewd; he wanted our discussion to move forward only cautiously. He knew I might do anything, so he kept bringing me back to the unacceptable idea of supreme sacrifice. Adults always have this fantasy of murdering their children, and some of them even act it out. Others make do with killing them every night in their dreams.

'. . . not a Jew or a Christian! And are there any other nice things you could tell me in your revolting stupid way?'

142

'I can't say anything if you keep interrupting. Try to control yourself. . .'

'I *am* controlling myself. Go on, but spare me the chorus – it's irrelevant.'

The room's darkness made my words sound strange. I felt as if they came out heavily, fell and stuck in the ground, over-burdened with contempt. Father spoke, and his phantom voice came to me from far away:

'Well. Your mother was perfect as a mother but distant as a wife. I've no intention of reading you the Zabor. I know you judge me harshly: that's your right, and I've no intention of getting out of it or justifying myself. I only want you to understand. . .'

The monster! The calm tone of his hollow words was so astonishing that I relaxed and started listening. But I had to interrupt and stop him lying any more:

'The camel never sees its own hump. You can't talk about Mi without criticizing her, even to strangers. I know you: you hate her. You always hated her, and us too. You weren't a proper husband yourself, or an ideal father. You were like all men of your sort: narrow and unbending, and arrogant at the same time. You are the model patriarch with a model house-hold: a cartoon called "the Driss family".'

I was just in time. Any longer and he would have got the upper hand, and that would have been intolerable. As long as I was speaking his eyes never left my feet, sticking out from under the blanket. I crossed my legs again to cover my feet. He continued:

'You know the mountain doesn't need the mountain, but. . .'

'*We* don't need *you* any more. You are nothing but a bad memory. . .'

He frowned. I used his surprise to bind him more tightly in my teeming thoughts:

'If you think I came all the way here to listen to your lies, you are wrong! I'm not here to kiss your hand and this is not a social visit. . .'

'You came to condemn me, I know, you said so before. . .'

His calmness exasperated me. Despite the tension between us and my burning words, he was still ice-cold. I was furious. You could feel it, and it was plain to see. I talked to avoid thinking:

'That's not true! You're afraid of me, old man. Afraid I'll get up and break your rotten bones with a hammer, afraid I might even piss on you and spit in your face, just like you when you humiliated me in front of other people, especially Nicole! Admit you are afraid *I* will treat *you* like a dog and smash your face! You are afraid I'll go back and tell Mi how miserably you live; you are afraid she'll say: "God's will!" and pray to the Lord of All to push you deeper into the shit. You are afraid – admit it! Right now, you turd, you are afraid of me. Admit you are afraid of us all, you are nothing but a coward, a villain, a . . .'

A violent gust of wind carried away my words. No need to worry. They flashed brightly enough to survive any good will or forgiveness. I stretched my legs. He stared at them. I folded them back under my body. He was in trouble. I went on:

'You sold the monkey to a Frenchman. That changed things for it. And you threw us into the street, and want me to understand – even forgive you, kiss your hand as before and beg your forgiveness. You are monstrous! All fathers are monstrous!

There was not much time left. I had to get him on his knees by dawn. He opened his mouth and I saw his gleaming dentures. The room was changing colour.

'You shouldn't have come. You are still only a child and there are some things in life you cannot understand. . .'

I was beside myself. His speech echoed like an insult in the cold room . He would not acknowledge that I was a man now and could fight grown-ups' degeneracy. That was why he did not react to my hatred: kid that I was, he would excuse this as a moment of childish hysteria. I had a few hours left to slay the dragon. I had to be cool and make him give in, never mind how. I had to submit him to my just distortions and make him admit his crime against us. Luckily I understood his tactics and was on my guard: he was trying to diminish me, to eliminate me more easily. He would not succeed; I was alert and determined to see this through to the end, determined to exterminate the Beast's complacence. The only way not to be corrupted by his insinuations was to stop him speaking:

'You know I am already twenty and strong enough to gouge out your eyes or split your skull. You know you're a monster who failed as a father and husband. You know you deserve nothing but our hatred and indifference. You know you've gone mad and enjoy multiplying yourself in your criminal procreation. You know all this – and you dare treat me like a child?'

He was staring at the wall. I felt I had never known this man, never seen him until now: a stranger who had murdered my life and was probably waiting for me to gouge out one of his eyes. I had to choose words that would explode in his face when I released them. Each word must snare him a little more firmly in repentance. He was calm and my task was difficult. I even believe he was expecting my blast of hatred, spurting out in violence and sincerity. I had managed to make him uncertain of his position and I kept bombarding him:

'Poverty and neglect – that was our lot! We were street-children, and that was your fault. Your itching penis condemned us to destruction. Wind – that is all you gave us. We're wind, nothing more, and we pass by without a trace. You carved holes in our memories and when you left we quietly vomited up our guts in the square and went away. . . We have done without them ever since. They stank of putrid father and crime. You were far away. You were between other legs, seeking oblivion in the abyss. . . We packed up time with our other luggage and went to rot somewhere else. Heaven watched for a moment in surprise, then slammed behind us. Our night became dreadful. You were far away in space, lost on the line of time. You drowned your memories in women who opened for your money or your madness. . . You've forgotten. You've forgotten yourself and your foul body fell into the

145

peaceful nothingness of the dead while we were drivelling on the unknown road of chance. It wasn't easy. If you think it was easy. . .'

Day was breaking and a twenty year old 'child' talked in the shadows. The other kept his eyes on my feet. I had to kill the dog before sunrise and the muezzin's call for first prayers.

But the road was still long and I was growing sleepy. My fingers were clenched on the wheel, paralysed with cold. And I still had to go on. At last he dared look at me and I knew he would break soon.

'God tells you to be good and generous to your wife and children. You failed in your duty to us. Have you really grown so stupid that you disobey the All Powerful? Are you so blind that you are ready to step out of line? Are you really mad enough to leave the right way laid down by Allah for the faithful? You won't be forgiven: you are done for and will choke on your own rage. I remember your hard words and fists and your impossible behaviour. There wasn't any drinking-water in the house – a waterless life! Hafid and I had to fetch fresh water from Titahcen all year round. Sometimes through the slaughterhouse at night, surrounded by carcasses and blood. It was good work for children. Coming back every night with bloodstained hands. One night you all but beat my brother to death with your belt. He had an essay to write and forgot to fill the buckets. After all, you gave us life so that we'd be good for something! I thought time would put everything right and God would see us one day and take pity on us. Nothing of the sort. We're still waiting, while you – you fly from cunt to cunt like a grotesque butterfly. It's your fourth divorce, they say. . . I can see Mi now, drowning in blood after the last birth. You were lost between whores' legs while she was fighting not to be torn apart. You were thinking: "She won't make it this time. Her womb is worn out with copulation and pregnancy. She won't make it. . ." You were evil and calculating. With that fatal confinement death would set you free to marry another woman, younger and more beautiful than Mi. And at nightfall you would forget yourself in her body and wake us from our shivering sleep with your howl: "She won't survive – the baby will strangle her – suffocate her. She'll carry my liberator in her womb. . ."

'You told yourself: "This time it's the end! I must be away on the day, forget to send for a midwife, make sure we're quarrelling with the neighbours. . ." You had an excuse: the monkey. You claimed their son had thrown a stone at it. We became official enemies. You were pleased. Every neighbour had his petty pride, so we squabbled about nothing at all. Loneliness – four walls and us. Then, the cold. Words made no sense and the sun was hiding behind the darkness. It was only a matter of days. You were using your old hypocritical smile, and talked about having a great party for the baptism. You rediscovered a fraction of your old tenderness for Mi and that threw you. Mi was condemned to death but hung on to life because of that deceptive warmth which vanished as soon as the baby was born. It was dead , but Mi was safe. You had been tricked and became as intolerable as before. You murdered your son and the crime was premeditated. . .'

The road streaked beneath me and I could see the lights glittering on a distant plateau. I was coming to my destination. My fingers were numb with cold. The windscreen wipers gradually swept away my memories as I drove into the night. Father still stared obsessively at my feet. He spoke without daring to look at me.

'My children all died after the last storm. You are only a stranger in my memory and you come here to crush me with your words. I have been dead too from the day I uprooted myself and abandoned my memories and my family. . .'

I was not listening. There was nothing left to listen to. I wasn't there to hear words: I had nothing to do with other people's words. Only my own mattered to me. I had to obliterate him before dawn and abandon him to remorse and old age.

The lights sharpened as I approached. Before they scattered

into the night I had to stop the dream of power which still lingered in that corrupt body. His words fell cold into the night and died:

'I sold all my possessions and sank alone in doubt and confusion, writhing alone in my madness. Your mother shed few tears. She thought I would die. They were lucid, hopeful tears. She forgot I had a pact with death. Death was too cold to catch me. I was dead to you that night and you buried me in a cracked wall: the wall of your conscience where I still wander like a shapeless dream. You could have saved me, saved us all by telling me that night. Now words flow by like time flowing. Only the night remains and when that has gone, only loneliness and remorse. . .'

He was cheating because he still would not look me in the eye. His motives were transparent and elusive. He was trying to make me submit to his madness and take pity on him and pardon his sins, but I could not forgive or pity. I didn't give him a chance to continue:

'I haven't come to hear your lying "philosophy". You must listen to me! You know I only have tonight to put these things straight. So shut up and listen! You ranted enough when I was little and the time has come to hear other people. . .'

He was still calm, not even raising his eyes. Surely he anticipated my every move. I knew how calculating he was. He would certainly have examined the affair from every side and prepared his defence. Hence his composure. I continued:

'And this is my final charge: you never taught us to laugh! Our life was a heap of iron prohibitions. We don't know how to laugh so we don't know how to live. We travelled through the strange passion of your past life. We shall never be happy if we don't know how to laugh. Hell lay in wait for us: the hell of callous faces, stripped words, shame, madness, obedience to tradition and the family, to words and gestures. The sun could rise or set, the moon could die on the sand, the bird could perish of shame and exhaustion – none of those things existed in our world. We were nailed like sin to the melancholy of the past. And laughter was forbidden. You prepared us

148

badly for this life of lies and corruption, this arid life withered by hearts' hatred. You always cheated us with cold calculation and profit. And kept Mi imprisoned. You were nothing but a monstrous ego, a monster who didn't know how to look at a tree or talk to a child, a brute like all the others, and we grew up with your lies in constant uncertainty and fear of the void. . .'

I spoke quickly, much too quickly. I did not want him to grasp the meaning of my words so I spoke headlong, wildly. I was only there after all to prove I could speak and reach him with my words.

He had been expecting me when I arrived at his house. We did not shake hands or even look at each other. He shut the door behind us and pointed to the single bed. He tried to take the lead by speaking first, and I let him. I wanted him to think I still respected the patriarch – that he was master of the situation as of old – so the fall would be more terrible. But he had foreseen everything. And what if I got up now and spat in his face or broke his skull with the pestle by the bed?

A lorry blazed my windscreen with its headlamps, and I nearly lost control of my thoughts. The ditch was deep and the night pitch black. Again the windscreen wiper swept away my fear and again the road glimmered before me. The rain had stopped.

A shadow on the back wall took human shape and stretched at my feet like a dog I might have been dragging behind me all my life. That dog knew me well: we were the same sort, he and I. I looked at it tenderly and felt more confident with it there. My feet were no longer cold. I continued:

'You are the son of the Devil and Aïcha Qandischa. Hell is ready to welcome you: the wages of sin. We have separated you off in the maze of our lives. You are only a dusty legend, oblivion can dislodge you at a hint from time. We were your goats but blood flowed one day, and we had died for you. But now we have killed you in our memories. Mi wept behind her veil. It was wet with tears and clung to her transparent cheeks. . .'

149

I saw Mi laid out on the ground, bare and cold. She did not move. Hafid and I stood by the door to accept the mourners' condolences. Hafid was crying. I struggled against the cold that shook my body. The weather was oppressive and reminded me of the burial of Messaouda. Around the corpse the aunts and cousins clawed their faces, tore their hair and beat their breasts. No one could accuse them of not living up to the occasion. On the *seddari* the *tolba* were hurriedly reading the prayers, while the weepers on the *seddari* opposite were putting on a fine display. The women who were not of the family also wept freely. Probably thinking of their own misery. They all made an unbearable racket. The beggars were eating the funeral couscous in the kitchen. I wanted to piss on the whole lot and throw them out. Too much hypocrisy and cowardice. I held back out of respect for Mi's soul.

Three days later the same show would be on the road again. The *tolba* and the weepers would come back. The family would gather again for the funeral supper and Mi would fall into eternal oblivion.

Father arrived in the midst of our grieving, supported by one of his brothers. He was blind drunk and had come to remind us of his contempt. He hated Mi and did not conceal his delight, cursing her soul and thanking heaven for avenging him before his own death. He danced around the coffin. There was a venomous silence. His brother restrained him as long as he could, then left him to his sad antics. My fingers tightened on the safety catch in my jacket pocket. I bit my lip till it bled. Father started raving:

'This is my revenge. . . hic. . . I told you so. Give me your condolences for the pious woman. . . hic. . . this proves she was wrong. She led us a dog's life. . . hic. . . God paid her back. She never listened to me. She's damned like her children. . . hic. . . She set them against me, their own father. . . hic. . . they wouldn't kiss my hand in the morning. They're all damned. She forgot I was "Cherif", the Prophet's descen-

150

dant. God let me see their misery. This is just the beginning. You'll see, you'll see much worse yet! Anyone who hurts me is punished by Allah. . . hic. . . the All Powerful. I prayed every morning for her to be punished – and she has been punished! Look at these planks. . . hic. . . hiding a festering corpse. . .'

I could take no more. Knife in hand, I threw myself at him and struck once, twice, three times. . .

I braked hard and just avoided swerving into the ditch. My nightmare slowly ebbed away and Father was lost again in the labyrinth of my oblivion.

Now the lights of peace and falsehood shone down on me, unfurling along the shining, rain-wet tarmac, and I erased them with the accelerator. The grey wall rose like perjury and locked the little village in its obsessive lust and madness. Behind me, a black hole and vague memories. Anxiety along the narrow streets, and at the end – a slow death, mysterious and cold.

A small, low house with all the unhappiness in the world inside. I reached the end of my long journey. Night had already fallen. My father stood stiff as death by the door of the little house of obsessions and aborted dreams. He was bare-headed, staring at the sky. A night full of bitterness. I walked over to him. He didn't even look at me. Still so proud and so mediocre. I was suddenly longing to be gone. . . too late! He was already holding out his heavy hand, which I kissed as of old.

His daughter was at his side, smiling at me, and speech was back in the cemetery of words.

Glossary

Aïcha Qandischa   an ogress of Moroccan folklore and legend
Aïd el Kebir   the great festival when sheep are sacrificed
aïta   a card game
Allah Akbar   God is great
aoulidi   my child
Azrou   a small town in the Middle Atlas of Morocco
Ba   father
Bslemah!   Thanks to God!
burnous   a cape with a hood
chergui   a fierce east wind
chikhats   female singers and entertainers
Chleuh   a Berber of the Atlas and ante-Atlas
chqaf   the clay bowl of a kif pipe
Ch'rif, chorfa   (s. and pl.) an honorific and sacred title given
    to direct descendants of the Prophet Mohammed
dahir   law
dekka   tea or other other liquid sipped while smoking kif
dirham   Moroccan currency
djellaba   long robe or cloak with hood
djinn, djinnoun   (s. and pl.) spirit, 'genie'
douar   a group of dwellings
Essaouira   Moroccan coastal town and port
falaqa   corporal punishment in which both feet are bound to
    a stick, and the soles beaten with another stick
Fassi   an inhabitant of Fez
fondouq   an inn or caravanserai
fqih   teacher and healer at religious schools

ghassoul   a kind of clay used as a shampoo

haïk   a large square of wool or linen which completely covers the female wearer

hammam   baths

harka   a ritualistic fantasia performed on horseback, involving the firing of rifles

hizb   communal recitation of religious text

houri   beautiful maiden promised by the Koran to the faithful and just in paradise

imam   a male reader or lecturer who leads the Muslim prayers

Incha'allah!   God willing!

Ismaïl   sultan

Istiqlal   the party of the independence movement in Morocco

J'ha   a legendary simpleton who always outwitted those who ridiculed him

Jihad   Muslim holy struggle, equivalent in meaning and connotation to 'crusade', except that it retains its original, non-metaphorical meaning and force

kanoune   a primitive chimney or fireplace made with three large stones

khammass   a peasant who, on feudal lines, receives from the landlord a fraction (a fifth) of the profits from the land he works

kif   the cleaned and cut leaves of the cannabis plant

latif   mercy (Abdelatif – slave of the Merciful)

Maghzen   the government

mansouria   woman's robe

medersa   school of Koranic theology, now by extension any school

medina   old Arab town, or quarter of a town

Mellah   the Jewish quarter

moqqaddem   a man acting as proctor for a given quarter of a town

Moulay Brahim   the site of an annual pilgrimage, in the foothills of the High Atlas

Moulay Driss   a small town in the Djebel Zerhoun

moussem   annual pilgrimage

m'sid   Koranic school

niqui   fuck (adapted from the French 'niquer')

nouiba   homosexual act in which each of two partners sodomizes the other, in turn

qadi   judge

Qadr   the 27th night of Ramadan is the night of Qadr – the Night of Destiny or Night of the Decree, when the Koran 'was sent down as a guidance for the people' (2:185) – when the heavens open to receive the supplications of the believers

qaouad   pimp

qoubba   a saint's tomb

Ramadan   the ninth month of the Muslim year, the Holy Month, throughout which a strict fast is observed by all pious Muslims between sunrise and sunset

Roumia   Christian/European woman

ronda   a card game not unlike rummy

sebsi   a kif pipe

seddari   a bench

s'hor   the third and last meal of the night, eaten before dawn, during the month of Ramadan

Si   a prefixed title implying respect

Sidi   used in everyday conversation, it means simply 'sir'. Coupled with a praenomen, it signifies a religious leader

Sidna Issa   Jesus, one of the Muslim prophets

souak   walnut bark, used by women to clean their teeth

souq   market, market stall

surah, surat   (s. and pl.) verse of the Koran

talaq   repudiation

taleb, tolba   (s. and pl.) student of divinity

tarbouche   any form of hat

tarha   loaves, arranged one on top of the other in the bread oven

tayaba   proprietress of the hammam

zakate   a levy on wealth

zaouya   burial place of a saint

zib   penis

Blec le Roc and *Miki the Ranger* are perennial French cartoon characters

Monsieur Séguin's Goat is a classic French children's book by Alphonse Daudet (1840-97)